COSTA RICA

COSTA RICA

BY DEBRA A. MILLER

LUCENT BOOKS

An imprint of Thomson Gale, a part of The Thomson Corporation

972.85
MIL

Detroit • New York • San Francisco • San Diego • New Haven, Conn. • Waterville, Maine • London • Munich

On cover: The city of San José, Costa Rica

© 2005 Thomson Gale, a part of The Thomson Corporation.

Thomson and Star Logo are trademarks and Gale and Lucent Books are registered trademarks used herein under license.

For more information, contact
Lucent Books
27500 Drake Rd.
Farmington Hills, MI 48331-3535
Or you can visit our Internet site at http://www.gale.com

ALL RIGHTS RESERVED.
No part of this work covered by the copyright hereon may be reproduced or used in any form or by any means—graphic, electronic, or mechanical, including photocopying, recording, taping, Web distribution or information storage retrieval systems—without the written permission of the publisher.

Every effort has been made to trace the owners of copyrighted material.

LIBRARY OF CONGRESS CATALOGING-IN-PUBLICATION DATA

Miller, Debra A.
    Costa Rica / by Debra A. Miller.
        p. cm. — (Modern nations of the world)
Includes bibliographical references and index.
ISBN 1-59018-623-0 (hardcover : alk. paper)
1. Costa Rica—Juvenile literature. I. Title. II. Series.
F1543.2.M55 2005
972.8605'2—dc22

                                                            2004028560

Printed in the United States of America

CONTENTS

INTRODUCTION

A NATION OF PEACE AND DEMOCRACY

Unlike many of its neighbors in Latin America, Costa Rica is remarkable for its long history of peace, stability, and democracy. In the sixteenth century Costa Rica, along with much of the rest of Central America, became part of the powerful Spanish colonial empire that developed in that region. By the nineteenth century, the Central American colonies had begun to rebel against Spanish rule. Instead of falling into a pattern of civil wars and military dictatorships like many of its Latin neighbors, however, Costa Rica chose democracy. It adopted a democratic constitution as early as 1823, soon after it declared its independence from Spain, and quickly held elections for its first legislature. In the early years of its independence, Costa Rica was part of a loose federation of neighboring nations, but it soon broke away from the federation to become a fully independent country.

TOWARD DEMOCRACY

Admittedly, the first several decades of Costa Rica's independence were not marked by a high degree of political stability. During this period, candidates supported by wealthy coffee growers governed the country, some even ruling as undemocratic and repressive dictators. Before the end of the nineteenth century, however, Costa Rica reached a point where it opted for greater democracy. This occurred in 1889, when, for the first time, a candidate not supported by the coffee elites won the presidential election. From this point onward, Costa Rica began to transition to full democratic rule.

Another important turning point came in 1948, when Costa Rica fought a civil war over disputed presidential election results. The fighting led to the adoption of a new constitution in 1949, which laid the foundation for the country's modern democratic state. Some of the most important parts of this constitution, for example, provided for the separation of powers between the executive, legislative, and judicial branches of government; free and fair elections; and universal voting rights for all citizens, including women. With this development, historians say that Costa Ricans renewed their dedication to the ideals of representative, democratic government and peaceful transfers of power. Since then, the country has reliably held nonviolent, democratic elections every four years. Today, because of this history, Costa Rica is recognized everywhere as one of the world's most stable democracies.

KEEPING THE PEACE

Costa Rica has also established an international reputation as a peaceful country. In fact, it is one of the few nations in the world without a military. The Costa Rican army was abolished in 1948, after the country's short civil war, as a way to

Costa Rican children march with flags during a 2004 Independence Day parade. After achieving independence from Spain in 1821, Costa Rica adopted a democratic constitution.

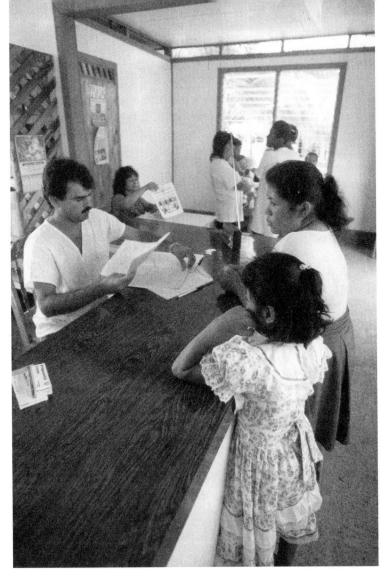

Patients check in at a health clinic in northeastern Costa Rica. Costa Ricans enjoy access to a variety of social services, including comprehensive health care.

prevent military coups from taking power and uprooting Costa Rica's precious democratic values. Instead, the government employs a police force to keep the peace domestically, and it has stayed neutral in disputes between other countries. This neutrality was threatened in the 1980s when its main trading partner, the United States, pressured the country to allow fighters (called Contras) opposed to the government in Nicaragua to establish bases in Costa Rica and conduct raids across the border. Yet even then Costa Rica, under the leadership of President Oscar Arias Sánchez, ultimately remained true to its peaceful ideals. Arias resisted the U.S. demands for cooperation with its military strategy and instead led the nations of Central America to sign a regional peace treaty that ended the civil war in Nicaragua as well as conflicts in other neighboring states. The success of the peace treaty earned Arias a Nobel Peace Prize in 1987. In 1993 Costa Rica proclaimed itself permanently neutral on the international stage.

ECONOMIC AND HUMANITARIAN ACHIEVEMENTS

Within its own borders, Costa Rica has promoted peace and stability among its citizens by redirecting funds that would otherwise have been spent on military forces into liberal social reforms. These reforms, begun as early as the late 1800s and consolidated in the post–civil war period of the 1940s, redistributed the nation's coffee wealth more widely among the population and provided citizens with generous education, health, and social security benefits. As a result of these reforms, Costa Rica has one of the highest literacy rates in the Western Hemisphere (97 percent), one of the best records on health care in the world, and the most secure and prosperous population in Central America. Also, as a society Costa Ricans have witnessed comparatively little ethnic or class conflict over the nation's century-plus existence. As a result of its human development programs and level of social security, in 1992 the United Nations removed the country from its list of underdeveloped nations.

In recent years Costa Rica's record of peace and prosperity has made it a haven for foreign investors seeking safe places to start up businesses or expand trade. Despite heavy foreign borrowing by the government and some downturns in its economy in recent decades, Costa Rica today is recognized as one of the best locations for investments such as technology and tourism. Both of these economic sectors are bringing new income into Costa Rica, allowing it to escape its historical dependence on just a few agricultural products, most notably coffee and bananas.

Peace and democracy have now become cherished traditions for Costa Ricans. As a people, Costa Ricans take great pride in their political and social accomplishments. This pride and self-confidence will no doubt help Costa Ricans to surmount whatever challenges lie ahead for the country.

1

LAND OF BEAUTY

In addition to its reputation for stability, Costa Rica is known around the world for the beauty of its environment and wildlife. Costa Rica is located on the Central American isthmus, the narrow strip of land that connects North and South America. The third-smallest country in the region (only El Salvador and Belize are smaller), Costa Rica occupies approximately 19,965 square miles, or a territory about the size of West Virginia. It measures about 300 miles from north to south, and at its narrowest point it is only about 74 miles wide. It is bordered on two sides by ocean—the Pacific Ocean to the west and the Caribbean Sea to the east. Nicaragua lies to the north, and Panama forms the country's southern border. Although small, Costa Rica is blessed with a wonderfully diverse and attractive natural environment—everything from tropical beaches to rich rain forests. Indeed, as sociology professor Richard Biesanz notes, because of its great beauty some have called the country the "Switzerland of Central America."[1]

COSTA RICA'S MOUNTAINS
Costa Rica's main geological feature is a string of mountain ranges that run north to south, splitting the country in half. The mountains are part of a volcanic range, the Cordillera de Guanacaste, that begins near Nicaragua and runs into another volcanic range, the Cordillera Central, which ends near the middle of Costa Rica. These two mountain ranges contain a spectacular chain of volcanoes, some of which are still active. These include the most active volcano in Costa Rica, Volcán Arenal, which has erupted almost constantly during recent years. Also located in the northern mountains is the Monteverde Biological Cloud Forest Reserve, a world-renowned, privately owned rain forest reserve and conservation area.

A third, higher, nonvolcanic range, the Cordillera de Talamanca, starts in central Costa Rica, runs through the southern part of the country, and continues into Panama and

Columbia. The Talamanca mountains are extremely rugged and contain some of the country's highest peaks. For example, Cerro de la Muerte reaches more than 11,400 feet, and the highest peak, Chirripó Grande, soars to 12,536 feet.

Costa Rica's mountains separate the country into three geographical regions—a narrow coastal lowlands region on the Pacific coast, an area of central highlands, and a somewhat wider coastal plain on the Caribbean side of the country.

THE PACIFIC COAST REGION

The Pacific coast region is a relatively narrow corridor of coastal lowlands. It is characterized by sandy beaches, steep cliffs, and numerous rock outcroppings. This western coastline is jagged, with numerous gulfs, peninsulas, and islands. The two most important peninsulas are the Nicoya Peninsula, which is located in the north and forms the large Nicoya Gulf, and the Osa Peninsula, which lies in the south and creates the

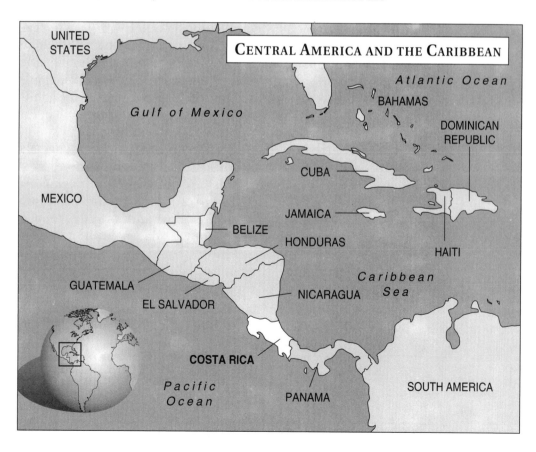

THE MONTEVERDE CLOUD FOREST RESERVE

The Monteverde Biological Cloud Forest Reserve, located in Costa Rica's northern mountains, is one of the largest privately owned nature preserves and wildlife sanctuaries in the world. It was founded in the 1950s by a small community of American Quakers who were attracted to Costa Rica because of its dedication to peace. The Quakers decided to create a nature preserve, and over the years they purchased additional land. In 1972 they joined with scholars from several universities to purchase even more forest land, and the area was given its present name and turned into a reserve dedicated to advancing scientific research. Today, the reserve spreads over 25,935 acres of land and contains incredible biodiversity. The reserve, for example, is home to at least 400 bird species, more than 100 species of mammals, 120 species of amphibians and reptiles, and an estimated 2,500 species of plants, including more than 400 species of delicate orchids. The reserve is open to tourists, and the tourist dollars are used to help preserve the forested area.

Golfo Dulce. The Nicoya Peninsula is dry with hilly terrain and is known for its cattle farming and beach resorts. The Osa Peninsula is much wetter and contains a national park, Corcovado National Park, which protects one of Costa Rica's rain forests. In addition, this southwestern part of the country is home to many of Costa Rica's banana plantations.

The Pacific side of Costa Rica's mountains is the site of tropical dry forests, a rare type of ecosystem that is sparsely vegetated, with far fewer tree species than the more common wet rain forests. Here, the canopy trees are deciduous rather than evergreen. The trees are short, often no more than 590 feet high, with strong trunks and large, flat-topped crowns. Underneath the canopy is another layer of smaller trees and a profusion of thorny shrubs instead of the lush vegetation often found in wet rain forests. The tropical dry forest is created by a lack of rain. On this side of the mountains, it does not rain for half the year, from November through March, yet vegetation is still exposed to relentless sun. The rains come in the spring, drenching the area. The water stimulates a dramatic response from the region's trees and plants, which produce an array of bright and colorful blooms. Flowering plants include the purple jacaranda, pink-and-white meadow oak, yellow *corteza amarilla*, scarlet *poró*, and the bright orange flame-of-the-forest.

Dry forests at one time covered all of the Pacific coastal lowlands. Today, however, they grow only in about 2 percent of their former range. Those that remain are endangered and threatened especially by fires, which can quickly wipe out an entire forest and replace it with opportunistic weeds and grasses. In this way, the forest is eventually turned into a grassland savannah. Much of northwest Costa Rica today consists of large expanses of these grassy savannahs, often dotted with grazing cattle.

THE CENTRAL HIGHLANDS AND VALLEY

The central highlands region forms the spine running down the middle of Costa Rica. Situated between two mountain ranges in this region is a large, fertile basin called the Central Valley. The valley is formed at the place where the Cordillera Central range connects with the Cordillera de Talamanca range. The Central Valley is enormous, measuring

A tourist takes in the scenery of one of the few remaining areas of dry tropical forest on the Pacific side of Costa Rica.

about thirty-nine hundred square miles, with an average altitude of more than three thousand feet.

The flattest part of the Central Valley is a central plateau called the Meseta Central. Soils in this area are rich and rain is abundant, creating lush vegetation. It is here that the country's capital city, San José, and most major cities are located, and where most of the country's population lives. This part of the Central Valley is also the site of much of the country's agricultural economy, which historically has been dominated by the coffee crop. Elsewhere in the Central Valley, in a basin called the General Valley in the south, the terrain is much less flat and more rugged. These areas are more hilly, covered with patches of woodlands, some crops, pastures, and numerous streams.

The central highlands region is the home of Costa Rica's famous tropical cloud forests—rain forests that grow in the clouds at elevations above three thousand feet. The moist environment here nourishes trees and a wide variety of plant, bird, and animal species. Above the rain forest areas is yet another ecosystem, called the *páramo*. The *páramo* is a high-altitude environment that contains only a few scrubby trees and is characterized instead by a variety of hardy shrubs and grasses. Chirripó Grande, Chirripó National Park, and the Cerro de la Muerte (Mountain of Death) are the principal areas of *páramo* in Costa Rica.

THE CARIBBEAN COAST

Unlike those on the Pacific side, the eastern mountain slopes on the Caribbean side of Costa Rica are broad and gentle. They extend into wide lowlands that cover almost one-fifth of the country's total land area. In contrast to the terrain found in the mountains and on the Pacific seaboard, the land here is marked mainly by flat plains, sandy beaches, and tidal marshes. Some lowlands in the northern part of the region, however, have a few hills and volcanoes. Another difference noticeable in this region is the near-constant precipitation, which creates high humidity. The rain also irrigates numerous streams that flow from the central highlands through the Caribbean lowlands.

Although more isolated and less developed than other parts of Costa Rica, this part of the country boasts beautiful beaches and pristine national parks and is becoming increasingly more popular as a surfing and tourist destination. Located here, for example, are two of the country's most popular national parks—Tortuguero National Park, which is one of the most important nesting grounds of the green sea turtle, and Cahuita National Park, which contains spectacular coral reefs. An excellent, world-renowned surfing spot is also found here, in a dusty little village called Puerto Viejo de Talamanca.

The Caribbean region is relatively unpopulated compared to other regions of Costa Rica. The largest city here is Limón, or Puerto Limón, a Caribbean port city. Most other settled areas consist of small towns and villages located near the coast, where life is unhurried and people generally adopt a friendly

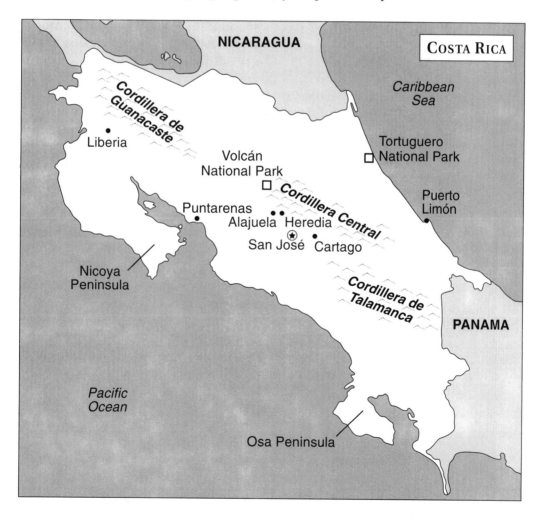

and laid-back attitude. Many of the nation's ethnic minorities live in this region, including most of the black population and several other groups such as indigenous peoples and some Chinese immigrants.

POPULATION AND CITIES

Costa Rica is home to almost 4 million people, the majority (or about 66 percent) of whom live in the central highlands area. In these urban areas, the population is quite dense, with people living in close proximity to each other. San José, the nation's capital, for example, sprawls over the heart of this area, and almost one-third of the nation's total population lives either in the city or in its large suburbs. San José is the political, business, and cultural center of Costa Rica, and the country's main transportation hub. From here, travelers can catch planes or buses that travel to locations outside and throughout the country. Although it was founded as early as 1737, the city's architecture does not appear to be colonial or quaint. Instead, San José is a modern, bustling, and very cosmopolitan city with high-rise buildings, numerous department stores, shopping malls, fast-food restaurants, museums, restaurants, and traffic problems. In recent years the government has improved some seedier parts of the city, bulldozing unattractive blighted sections, removing unsightly telephone lines, and creating several beautiful parks.

Sprinkled around San José in the highlands area are numerous other cities and towns. Some of the largest and most notable of these are Alajuela, Heredia, and Cartago. Alajuela, located just northwest of San José, is said to be a smaller version of the capital city. With a population of about 35,000, it is somewhat congested (especially on weekends), but it is relatively cosmopolitan with good museums, parks, and markets. Heredia, a city near Alajuela with about the same population size (32,000), is much less urban. Neat old adobe houses, colonial architecture, and narrow streets complement the slow-paced atmosphere. Heredia is also the site of Costa Rica's National University, which is famous particularly for its veterinary program. The city of Cartago, located southeast of San José, was Costa Rica's first city. It was founded in 1563 by Spanish settlers and became the area's colonial capital. In a population of 26,400, many citizens can trace their ancestors back to the founding families of the

This is a view of downtown San José, Costa Rica's bustling capital city that is home to nearly one-third of the country's population.

Cartago settlement, and today it still is considered the country's most traditional and religious city. Despite the city's historical roots, however, few old buildings have survived due to the area's many earthquakes.

Several other major cities can be found outside of Costa Rica's highland region. These include two cities in the Pacific coastal region—Liberia and Puntarenas. Liberia is the largest city in the far northwest of the country. As travel writer Christopher P. Baker notes, "It is called 'the White City' because of its houses made of blinding white ignimbrite [a hard rock made from volcanic deposits]."[2] Liberia is also the area's main economic and transportation hub, bringing visitors to the nearby resorts of the Nicoya Peninsula. Also in the northern Pacific lowlands area, but south of Liberia, is the port town of Puntarenas, which means "Sandy Point." The town's name comes from its location; it is built on a long, narrow peninsula only five blocks wide, which juts out from the mainland. Puntarenas is the main population center on the

Pacific coast and is only about seventy-five miles west of San José. Once the main port used by the Spaniards, today it is home to fishermen and is used mainly as a departure point for ferries and cruises to sites in the Gulf of Nicoya.

Limón (also known as Puerto Limón) is the only large town on the Caribbean coast and is now Costa Rica's main port city. It has four docks, including a new port for large cruise ships, and it handles most of the sea trade coming in and out of the country. *Limón* means "Lemon," and the city acquired the name because a big lemon tree once grew at the site of its town hall. Despite its maritime importance and size (population of sixty-five thousand), however, Limón has been described as sleazy and run-down due to its many decayed buildings and lack of public improvements. It also has developed a reputation as a center for drug traffic and crime, and it is not typically frequented by tourists.

Automobiles, bicycles, and pedestrians share a street in Liberia, one of the major cities located outside Costa Rica's highland region.

CLIMATE AND WEATHER

Although Costa Rica lies entirely within the tropics, its weather is greatly affected by its geology. Temperatures and rainfall are determined largely by elevation. On the coasts, temperatures are warmer (typically averaging between eighty to ninety degrees Fahrenheit) with light rainfall amounts. Mountainous areas and the Central Valley, on the other hand, average around seventy-two degrees, with daytime temperatures reaching as high as eighty-five degrees and dropping at night sometimes as low as a chilly sixty degrees. These higher elevation areas also get much more rain.

The country has only two main seasons, the rainy season (winter) and the dry season (summer). The rainy season usually lasts from May to November, and the wettest months are commonly in September and October. Often the days during this period begin sunny and cloudless but are quickly followed by overcast skies and rain. Rainstorms can range from a drizzle, to a brief downpour, to a steady, days-long storm. The dry season typically begins in mid-November or December, when strong north winds blow away the rain and humidity and bring warmer temperatures. The change in weather signals the beginning of the coffee harvest and the Christmas holiday season. During the first couple of months of the dry season, temperatures remain cool and most areas stay green. As the dry season progresses, however, the air gets much warmer and drier and many plants turn brown. By the end of the dry season in April, people long for the rains to come again. The rainstorms replenish the country's water supplies, create its numerous rivers and streams, and irrigate its rain forests and crops. The length of the seasons, however, are different for the various regions of the country. On the humid Caribbean slopes, for example, there is almost no dry season, while the Pacific coasts experience a very long dry period.

Costa Rica's climate and geology can sometimes turn destructive. Excess rain, for example, can cause flooding that can ruin crops, damage property, and cause injury or death. Drought, on the other hand, can also damage crops and create fire hazards. In addition, Costa Rica is located in an active seismic area, where earthquakes are common. Most earthquakes are small and extremely harmless, but strong earthquakes do occasionally occur. In 1991, for instance, an earthquake measuring 7.4 on the Richter scale hit the Caribbean side of the country. A third destructive natural force in Costa Rica is volcanic activity. The country has seven active volcanoes and sixty-nine dormant ones. The last big volcano eruption was in 1963, when the Irazú Volcano exploded after a twenty-year rest, showering San José with smoke and ash.

RIVERS AND RAIN FORESTS

Costa Rica's abundant rainfall is responsible for two of its natural wonders—rivers and rain forests. Most of the country's rivers begin in the central highlands region and flow to the east, toward the Caribbean Sea. Others flow westward to the Pacific Ocean. One important eastbound river, the San Juan, originates in Lake Nicaragua (inside the country of Nicaragua) before it flows into Costa Rica. The San Juan forms part of the border between the two countries. During its 124-mile course through rain forests and mountains, the San Juan unites with two other rivers, the San Carlos and the Sarapiquí, until it empties into the Caribbean Sea at the town of San Juan del Norte. Also flowing eastward is the Reventazón, a river that originates in the Cordillera de Talamanca mountain range, one of the wettest parts of Costa Rica. The Reventazón rushes through steep mountain areas and scenic jungles, and the river contains more than 60 miles of whitewater rapids, which are popular with tourists. Some of Costa Rica's eastern rivers have also been used for hydroelectric power. Rivers that flow toward the Pacific include the Río Grande de Tárcoles, which streams from the San José area westward, and the Río Grande de Térraba, which is located in the southern part of the Pacific coastal region and is the country's longest river.

Yet another wonder made possible by Costa Rica's climate is its tropical rain forests. Rain forests still cover a large portion of Costa Rica, mostly on the eastern coastal areas and a few southern Pacific slopes. These tropical rain forests are the richest and most diverse biological ecosystem on the planet. They contain a multitude of plant and animal species, some of which have yet to be discovered. As travel writer Baker describes, "Costa Rica alone has as many plant species as the whole of Europe, and the number of insect species in a hectare [2.47 acres] of rainforest is so great that no successful count has been made."[3]

VOLCANOES AND EARTHQUAKES

Costa Rica's great beauty is tempered by two destructive forces of nature—earthquakes and volcanoes. Because the country is located on a natural bridge between North and South America, an area where two plates of the earth's crust intersect, it is prone to tremors and earthquakes caused by slight movements of these plates. Fortunately, smaller earthquakes are much more common than serious ones. The last sizable earthquake occurred on April 22, 1991. It damaged much of the Caribbean side of the country and left twenty-seven people dead, four hundred injured, and thirteen thousand homeless. Due to the threat of earthquakes, Costa Rica has strict building codes for high-population areas like San José.

Another important Costa Rican geological feature is the volcano. The country's seven active volcanoes (and sixty-nine inactive ones) are part of a string of volcanic mountains, called the Pacific Rim of Fire, that spreads throughout Central America. Big volcano eruptions tend to be infrequent; most volcanoes appear as peaceful mountains in the distant landscape. Today, the country's most active volcano is the Volcán Arenal, a 5,366-foot peak that erupted for the first time in 1968 and since has been continually steaming, exploding, and spewing forth red-hot lava.

Costa Rica has several active volcanoes, including Volcán Arenal, shown here erupting in the distance beyond a rain forest.

Unfortunately, many of Costa Rica's rain forest areas have been deforested or are in the process of disappearing. Land has been cleared for pasture or agriculture, and other areas have been logged for their precious hardwoods. The rate of deforestation is, indeed, alarming: Three-quarters of the country was covered by forest in the 1940s, but by the 1990s only a fraction of this forest remained. Costa Rica today is aggressively trying to stop this process of decline.

THE QUETZAL:
COSTA RICA'S NATIONAL BIRD

One of the most famous birds in Costa Rica is the beautiful and elusive quetzal. A vivid, shimmering emerald green color, with a red belly and two-foot-long, bright green tail plumes edged in white, the quetzal is known around the world as one of the most spectacularly colored birds in the Western Hemisphere. In fact, the bird's name comes from *quetzalli*, an Aztec word meaning "beautiful," and the quetzal's feathers were one of the most important items traded by the Maya civilization of Central America. Over the years, the quetzal has become a symbol for Costa Ricans of their independence and freedom.

Today, it is still possible for visitors to see quetzal birds in Costa Rica's high-altitude cloud forests. The birds are very shy and are well camouflaged in the green rain forests, but they can often be seen feeding on fruit, nesting in dead trees, or displaying their feathers in flight.

The brilliantly colored quetzal of the rain forest has long been a symbol of Costa Rican independence.

FLORA AND FAUNA

Costa Rica's diverse ecology and abundant rainfall produce a variety of flora and fauna, both in its rain forests and in other parts of the country. In Costa Rica's tropical forests, for example, more than fourteen hundred tree species have been recorded. The country is also home to some ten thousand species of other plants, including orchids, which account for about twelve hundred different species. The most famous orchid type is the *Cattelya skinneri,* Costa Rica's national flower.

The incredible plant diversity provides a habitat for an equally amazing number and variety of animals, insects, fish, and birds. In fact, more than 850 bird species have been identified, more than are found in all of the United States and Canada. In addition, there are more than 200 mammal species, 220 types of reptiles, 130 kinds of freshwater fish, and at least 35,000 classified insect species. Many of these species are listed as endangered under Costa Rican law.

The best places to see Costa Rica's wildlife and other environmental treasures are in the country's many national parks and private preserves. Today, there are about eighty different national parks, wildlife refuges, and similar reserves and recreation areas set aside as protected areas. In addition, there are private-owned reserves and numerous buffer zones that are also protected from development. Visitors can enter most national parks, but private and other reserves often are off-limits without a special permit. Costa Rica, although small in size, clearly possesses priceless natural resources that the nation's people believe are worth protecting.

2

Costa Rica's Beginnings

Although colonized by Spain along with most of Central America, Costa Rica eventually was able to establish its independence. Unlike many of its neighbors in the region, however, Costa Rica largely avoided destructive political and social upheavals often sparked by struggles between the rich and the poor. Instead, the new nation slowly built its economy, set up generous social programs, and steered itself toward a stable and democratic future.

Early Inhabitants

Costa Rica's earliest inhabitants were nomadic hunters who traveled to the area as early as 12,000 B.C. Over a period of thousands of years, these nomadic people settled down to plant crops such as sweet potatoes, corn, and beans. These foods were supplemented by hunting and fishing. These early Costa Ricans lived in large family groups, or tribes, and the various tribes are believed to have numbered at one point as many as four hundred thousand people. Most of these people lived in the Central Valley, the home of most of Costa Rica's modern population, as well as in the northern Pacific area. They left many artifacts attesting to their existence.

The Costa Rican tribes formed trading relationships with Mexican and Mayan tribes from the north as well as other tribes from as far south as Ecuador. They traded items such as salt, cacao, feathers, and dyes. They also were skilled artisans who made jewelry and other objects out of jade and gold imported from outside areas. Much of this artwork reflected Mayan and other external influences. For the most part, however, these early Costa Ricans lived the lives of farmers, cultivating crops such as sweet potatoes, corn, beans, and cassava (a tropical plant grown for its starchy roots).

Yet unlike other civilizations of the time, such as the Mayans in Guatemala and similar areas, the tribes of Costa Rica did not erect large structures or build impressive cities. The explanation for this appears to be that these early tribes lived autonomously in local groups and were not organized together as part of a larger civilization. In fact, although they sometimes formed temporary alliances with neighboring tribes, archaeological remains suggest that the indigenous tribes frequently warred with each other. These divisions among the local tribes made it difficult for outsiders to dominate them since each individual group had to be conquered separately.

EUROPEAN CONQUEST AND THE COLONIAL PERIOD

The first European contact with the area came in 1502, when Spanish explorer Christopher Columbus landed at what is today the port of Limón, Costa Rica. Columbus reported seeing the indigenous people there wearing gold jewelry, and they gave him many gifts of gold. In search of more gold, Spain soon sent other explorers to the region, who were also given gold as presents. Because of the resulting excitement over the possibility of vast gold reserves in the region, Spain began calling the area Costa Rica (meaning "Rich Coast").

Early native Costa Rican peoples used a grindstone like this to grind corn, one of a few staple crops on which they subsisted.

Spanish expeditions over the next several decades to Costa Rica, however, found little gold that could be mined to enrich Spain. Instead, the neighboring mineral-rich area today known as Guatemala became Spain's main area of settlement in Central America. Nevertheless, Costa Rica also became a colony of Spain and part of a large Spanish Central American colonial empire administered from headquarters in Guatemala. Although the isolated settlements and fierce resistance of Costa Rica's indigenous groups at first made domination of the local population difficult for the Spaniards, by 1561 Spain had managed to establish an inland settlement in the Central Valley at Cartago. Later, additional Spanish settlements were established at Alajuela, Heredia, and San José.

For the local people, whom the Spanish called Indians, the colonial period basically meant the destruction of their way of life and sometimes even their death. As political science professor Bruce M. Wilson describes, "Of a population of 27,500 Indians in 1522, fewer than 15,000 remained less than a hundred years later, and that number had diminished to 8,281 by 1801."[4] Many native people were captured as slaves and were forced to work for the Spaniards in various colonies in the region. Most of the local population, however, was ravaged and killed by new diseases brought by the Spaniards. These included smallpox, typhoid fever, and measles. Some indigenous people survived by fleeing to remote forested areas where they could not be found by the Spanish settlers. Soon, the local labor pool had dwindled so much that the Spanish settlers were forced to farm their own lands without slave help. In fact, even the colonial governors of Costa Rica had to work their own lands. These conditions prevented the development of large, profitable plantations like those in other Spanish colonies and created instead a number of small, independent farms in Costa Rica.

The poverty of the settlers, together with the general isolation of the area and the failure to find exportable minerals or other products, made Costa Rica unimportant to Spain and a relatively neglected part of the Spanish colonial system. As Richard Biesanz describes, "Costa Rica has been called the Cinderella of the Spanish colonies, for it was taxed, scolded, ignored, and kept miserably poor."[5] Because of this neglect, a society evolved in the Central Valley during the

colonial period that had little contact with or allegiance to the Spanish administrators in Guatemala. It was this nucleus of rural, independent Spanish settlers that eventually formed the population of modern Costa Rica. This population was mostly of European ancestry. Although a few indigenous people, or Indians, formed their own villages in the Talamanca mountain area, most intermarried with Spanish settlers and merged into the Spanish culture.

In addition, the poverty and isolation of Costa Rica helped to delay development during the colonial period and preserve its natural resources. Unlike some other Spanish colonies, therefore, Costa Rica emerged from the colonial period with a small but peaceful agricultural society and with its environmental resources largely intact.

The Boruca Indians of Costa Rica perform an annual ritual dressed in costumes and masks dating to precolonial times.

INDEPENDENCE FROM SPAIN

In 1821 Costa Rica and what are now the nations of Nicaragua, El Salvador, Honduras, and Guatemala declared themselves independent from Spain. This group also claimed to be independent from Mexico, which had also broken away from Spain and envisioned itself as the leader of a broad Central American empire. Instead of joining Mexico, the group of five nations formed a federation, the United Provinces of Central America, and called for democratic elections and the abolition of slavery. In 1823 Costa Rica officially joined the federation. The federation, although it ultimately failed and was dissolved in 1838, provided a valuable model of unity and democratic rule. Costa Rica, for example, adopted a constitution and government that was modeled on the federation concepts of democracy. From this point on, Costa Rica progressed steadily to embrace even greater progressive and democratic ideals. Costa Rica's development contrasted with the path chosen by some other Central American countries, where competing political interests brought a cycle of civil wars and military governments that ruled by repression.

The ancestors of modern Costa Ricans, Spanish settlers on a plantation are shown spreading coffee beans to dry in the sun.

Costa Rica's first few decades of independence, however, were unstable and divisive, with many different leaders holding power. In 1824 a congress was elected, and it chose the country's first leader, Juan Mora Fernández, who ruled peacefully for nine years. Mora tried to unify Costa Ricans, expanded education, established the country's first judicial system, and started the country's first newspaper. He also encouraged coffee cultivation. In 1834, however, a new head of state, Braulio Carrillo Colina, was elected. When he lost his bid for reelection in 1838, he seized control of the government and ruled as a dictator. During his rule, the country's capital was moved to San José. Despite his autocratic methods, Carrillo also is credited with making useful improvements to Costa Rica's legal codes and with promoting coffee production through land grants and gifts of plants to the poor. Carrillo was toppled from power in 1842 by Francisco Morazán, but Morazán himself was overthrown when Costa Ricans discovered that he wanted to use the country as a base to invade other areas of Central America. During the next several years, multiple leaders held office. Finally, in 1847 the congress named José María Castro Madriz as president. Castro was a strong believer in press freedom and education, and he founded the first high school for girls. By this time, however, Costa Rica's coffee growers had risen to become very powerful politically. Castro was forced to resign in 1849 by a group of wealthy coffee growers who opposed his reforms. He was replaced as president by Juan Rafael Mora Porras, a coffee baron who was concerned mostly with staying in power and promoting the interests of the coffee industry.

Surprisingly, it was during this period of relative instability that Costa Ricans finally came together as a nation. This unity came not because of strong internal leadership, however, but in response to an external threat from an American adventurer, William Walker. Walker and his backers believed the United States could take control of other nations as part of a philosophy known as manifest destiny. Walker arrived in neighboring Nicaragua in 1855 with a private army funded mostly by a group of wealthy U.S. citizens. He immediately took control of the Nicaraguan government and declared himself Nicaragua's new president. By early 1856 Walker was poised to invade Costa Rica. At the urging of President Mora, however, Costa Ricans from all social classes rallied together to fight against Walker's soldiers, forcing them to retreat into Nicaragua. Many Costa Ricans died in the battles, including Pancha Carrasco, a female cook who joined the men on the battlefield. Another Costa Rican, a young soldier named Juan Santamaría, was shot while setting fire to an enemy stronghold; he is now celebrated as one of Costa Rica's national heroes. The victory over Walker helped to unite Costa Ricans and gave them a greater sense of national identity. As Biesanz explains, "For the first time Costa Ricans felt a sense of nationalism transcending old localist interests and grudges."[6]

TOMÁS GUARDIA AND THE GENERATION OF 1889

Despite the national unity inspired by fighting off Walker's invasion, coffee growers continued to be increasingly powerful in the country's politics. Many different coffee families competed for power, and for decades they were able to influence the election or removal of presidents as it suited their economic interests. This pattern ended in 1870 with the election of Tomás Guardia Gutiérrez, a popular but authoritarian president whose cause became curbing the power of the coffee barons. Guardia governed for twelve years as a dictator, destroying many of Costa Rica's democratic protections but at the same time weakening the power of the coffee interests by taking control of the armed forces and appointing new leaders to important government positions.

Guardia also made many other progressive improvements for the country. Most significantly, he instituted a program of taxes that allowed him to better the lives of ordinary Costa Ricans. With the tax proceeds, he improved education and public health. Guardia also began a program of public works that included construction of the country's first railroad. The railroad, in turn, spurred the country's economic development. Although built to transport coffee, the railroad also gave birth to a new banana industry, which used the railroad to transport bananas to market from the remote Caribbean coastal area of the country. Perhaps ironically, Guardia's dictatorial rule ushered in a long period of social and economic reform in Costa Rica that eventually led to the country's modern democracy.

After Tomás Guardia's death in 1882, a group of young men, called "the Generation of 1889," continued his work by

WILLIAM WALKER

William Walker, an American adventurer from Tennessee, played a major role in Costa Rica's history. Walker was a highly educated man with degrees in both law and medicine, but he was renowned as a soldier of fortune. Walker received funding from American industrialist Cornelius Vanderbilt as well as a group of U.S. slaveholders, and he began promoting both slavery and an American conquest of Latin America. Walker and his army arrived in Nicaragua in 1855 with two objectives: to convert Nicaragua into slave territory and to construct an eighteen-mile canal across the country, a project favored by Vanderbilt. Walker quickly defeated Nicaragua's army and declared himself president of Nicaragua. Costa Rican president Juan Rafael Mora, recognizing Walker's threat to Costa Rica, raised an army of nine thousand Costa Ricans from all walks of life in just a few days. This army marched to the Nicaraguan border, where a small group of Walker's troops attacked them. The battle was over in minutes, and Walker's soldiers were forced to retreat into Nicaragua. Walker ultimately failed to achieve his goals in Nicaragua, but he continued to cause trouble in Central America for several more years. He was finally executed in 1860 in Honduras after an attempt to gain control of that country.

pushing for even more progressive social change in Costa Rica. Indeed, the election of 1889 marked the first time in the country's history in which a candidate not supported by the coffee elites, José Joaquín Rodríguez Zeledón, won an election and was allowed to take office. This marked a milestone for the country's democratic system. Over the next few decades, social programs and public works were further expanded, religious freedoms were instituted, and democratic reforms were adopted. Two other national leaders, Cleto González Víquez and Ricardo Jiménez Oreamuno, are remembered fondly by Costa Ricans for their contributions during this period. González promoted public works and health care, and Jiménez tried to improve the voting system.

In 1917, however, a repressive coup took control under the leadership of Frederico Tinoco Granados. Tinoco ignored democratic reforms, violated citizens' civil rights and press freedoms, and filled the jails with political prisoners. Within

COSTA RICA'S FIRST RAILROAD

Costa Rican president Tomás Guardia was responsible for the building of Costa Rica's first railroad at the end of the nineteenth century. The railroad was necessary to provide a better method of transportation for the nation's coffee exports. Construction of a railroad had been financed in the 1870s by British banks, but the effort failed because of Costa Rica's difficult terrain. In 1883 Minor Cooper Keith, a wealthy American, approached the government of Costa Rica with an offer: Keith would build and finance the railroad with his own money if Costa Rica would give him 7 percent of the nation's territory for banana production. Guardia approved the deal, and construction of the railroad resumed. The humid conditions in the Caribbean lowlands were so difficult, however, that Costa Ricans would not do the work. Keith brought in workers from China and blacks from Jamaica to finish the job. The railroad was completed seven years later, in 1890, at a cost of five thousand workers' lives. Despite the great cost, the railroad improved transportation of Costa Rica's coffee and also helped to create an entirely new banana industry on the country's Caribbean coast.

In the early twentieth century, dockworkers at a port on the Caribbean coast load bananas from freight cars onto a cargo vessel.

a short time, Tinoco's rule became so oppressive that demonstrators comprised mostly of female schoolteachers rebelled by setting fire to a pro-Tinoco newspaper plant. Government troops controlled by Tinoco began firing on the demonstrators. Finally, with pressure from the United States, the Costa Rican congress intervened, and in 1918 it forced Tinoco to resign and flee into exile. This was Costa Rica's last military dictatorship.

Thereafter, the country began to make significant social and civic improvements under new, democratically elected leaders. By 1937, responding to growing problems such as poverty, health issues, and exploitation of workers in the fast-growing banana industry, the country had moved to adopt additional new social programs. Among these were programs that provided for free education that was made compulsory through the sixth grade, a maximum workday and a minimum wage, a commission to set salaries, accident insurance, industrial hygiene, and protections for mothers and children.

Social Reforms of the 1940s

Leaders in the 1940s greatly advanced Costa Rica's reform efforts, putting into place an even wider range of social protections. This process began with the election in 1940 of President Rafael Ángel Calderón Guardia. Calderón was supported by the coffee elite, but surprisingly he championed the rights of workers and the poor. He introduced reforms such as a program of social security (including unemployment, health, accident, and old-age benefits), an eight-hour workday, a minimum wage increase, and a labor code that protected workers' rights to organize and bargain collectively with their employers. As Bruce M. Wilson explains, Calderón "became the first president of Costa Rica to make 'genuine social and economic reform the primary goal of his administration.'"[7]

Calderón's actions won many supporters among workers and the fledgling middle class, while alienating landowners and big-business interests. Calderón, however, believed social protections were necessary to reconcile the interests of business and labor and to avoid class conflict in Costa Rica. Ultimately, Calderón succeeded largely by building a coalition, which included both the

Schoolgirls learn how to brush their teeth correctly, part of Costa Rica's ambitious social reform program that began in the 1940s.

Catholic Church and the Communist Party, to support his social and economic legislation. This coalition continued under a succeeding president, Teodoro Picado Mikalski. Picado was handpicked by Calderón and his supporters to carry on the reform efforts.

Calderón's and Picado's reforms, however, were strongly opposed by coffee growers and other business interests. The opposition pointed out that reforms were costly and produced a growing budget deficit. In addition, the reforms were instituted at a time when Costa Rica was already experiencing an economic downturn caused by World War II. As part of its cooperation with the U.S. side against Germany in the war, the government also took punitive actions against Costa Ricans of German descent, such as taking their farms and businesses and sending many to concentration camps. This affected many from the business community. Moreover, critics charged that Picado's election was fraudulent and that the Calderón-Picado government was tainted by widespread corruption. In 1947 Picado implemented new tax laws on businesses that proved to be the breaking point. The business-supported opposition staged demonstrations and businesses closed for a month, initiating a period of general civil unrest and violence in Costa Rica. A demonstration by thousands of Costa Rican women finally resolved the matter. The women demanded an end to the violence, and their demands led President Picado to sign an agreement with opposition leaders providing for election reforms.

THE CIVIL WAR OF 1948 AND JOSÉ FIGUERES'S JUNTA

The elections of 1948 triggered major changes in Costa Rica's government. Although a conservative candidate, Rafael Otilio Ulate Blanco, received the most votes, Calderón supporters in Congress annulled the results. This action quickly resulted in a civil war. Within months, insurgent fighters led by an ally of Ulate, José Figueres Ferrer, gained control of much of southern Costa Rica and were poised to take over the capital. Nicaraguan forces occupied the northern part of the country in support of Calderón fighters. Both sides thought they were fighting for the future of Costa Rica. As Biesanz explains, "*Calderonistas* thought they were fighting to preserve social reforms; *figueristas*, that they were . . . fighting corruption and communism."[8] By the spring of

JOSÉ FIGUERES FERRER

José Figueres Ferrer, affectionately called "Don Pepe" by Costa Ricans, was one of the most influential politicians in Costa Rican history. Born in 1906, he was largely self-educated during time spent in the United States in the 1920s. He became fascinated with the U.S. system of government, which he saw as providing for social justice within a free-enterprise economy. In the 1940s Figueres criticized President Rafael Ángel Calderón Guardia, an action that caused him to be exiled for two years to Mexico. While in Mexico, he became allied with newspaperman Rafael Otilio Ulate Blanco, and when Ulate was denied the presidency of Costa Rica in 1948, Figueres instigated civil war. Figueres then took control of the Costa Rican government, remaking it into its modern image. He abolished the army, established a broad system of social welfare programs, and rewrote the constitution to provide for free and fair elections and universal suffrage. He turned the government over to Ulate in 1949, but he later founded the National Liberation Party and was elected president himself on two occasions, in 1953 and 1970. Figueres is largely credited with leading Costa Rica into a new era of political stability and economic growth. He died in 1990.

José Figueres (center, wearing dark suit), pictured here with government soldiers, is regarded as the father of modern democracy in Costa Rica.

1948, about two thousand soldiers had already died in the uprising. Fortunately, negotiations began at this time to try to resolve the crisis. In April 1948 an agreement was signed that ended the fighting and provided for an interim president and a general amnesty for combatants.

Ultimately, however, Figueres ignored the agreement and made another deal with Ulate. Under this new pact, Figueres took control of the government through a revolutionary junta, or committee, ruling by decree for eighteen months. During this period, Figueres enacted 834 decrees that dramatically transformed the constitution and government of

Costa Rica. Some of these reforms gave women the right to vote and conferred full citizenship on previously marginalized groups, such as blacks living in the Caribbean region of the country. At the same time, Figueres banned the Communist Party, exiled other Calderón supporters, and reduced the number of unions. Most significantly, to prevent future destabilizing military coups (perhaps from exiled *Calderonistas* who had friends in the military), Figueres abolished the country's army. The junta government also nationalized the banking system, redistributed wealth through taxes on rich Costa Ricans, and further improved education and social security programs favored by Calderón. Figueres then handed over power to Ulate, whose election had sparked the country's civil war. Figueres went on to build a base of supporters who formed the National Liberation Party, which became the dominant political party in Costa Rican politics for the next forty years.

Although Figueres's methods have been criticized, most historians agree that his reforms and guidance set Costa Rica firmly on a path of social stability, peace, and democracy. As professor Marc Edelman and journalist Joanne Kenen put it, "Under [Figueres's] rule the wounds of the 1940s have largely healed and a more genuine, albeit imperfect, democracy has taken root [in Costa Rica]."[9]

DEMOCRATIC COSTA RICA

3

The 1948 civil war in Costa Rica was followed by decades of political stability, economic prosperity, and social achievements that gave the country a reputation around the world as a shining example of tranquility and democracy. Today, Costa Rica remains a bastion of democracy and peace, dedicated to providing for its citizens, even as it struggles with economic, environmental, and other challenges.

DECADES OF PEACE, DEMOCRACY, AND PROSPERITY

One important legacy of Costa Rica's civil war was restoration of fair elections and a rededication of Costa Ricans to the concept of representative government and peaceful transfers of power. The new constitution, adopted by an elected assembly in 1949, put in place new laws to enforce these goals and strengthen democracy in the country. As professor Bruce M. Wilson explains, "The new constitution, written in the aftermath of the [civil] war, marked the end of the old regime and laid the foundations of the modern Costa Rica state, including its electoral laws, distribution of political power, and the legal groundwork for increased state intervention in economic and social issues."[10] One of the most important electoral changes was the creation of the Supreme Electoral Tribunal, an independent, elected body that is charged with supervising elections and making sure they are peaceful and fair. Other electoral rules provided for presidential, legislative, and municipal elections every four years and universal voting rights for all citizens, including women and a small black population.

With these protections in place, on November 9, 1949, Rafael Otilio Ulate Blanco assumed the presidency without incident. During the next several decades, Costa Rica held numerous peaceful elections with high voter participation.

In these elections, presidential power alternated between Figueres's National Liberation Party (PLN) and an opposition party made up of various coalitions that have changed over the years. Figueres himself successfully ran for president in both the 1953 and the 1970 elections.

Another consequence of the war and Figueres's leadership was agreement among Costa Ricans that the government should provide social security for its citizens. Compared to the major changes enacted by Figueres, earlier social programs promoted by Calderón and Picado no longer seemed radical and were soon considered a part of the country's proud history. In addition, Figueres and other Costa Rican leaders were later able to greatly expand the Calderón protections. They devoted more funds to education, created low-income housing programs, and extended health care to

Supporters of Figueres stage a rally for him in 1953. Women voted for the first time in this election.

all citizens and all parts of the country. By the early 1980s, in fact, almost half the national budget was being spent on health care and another one-third on education. These efforts helped the country to achieve remarkable improvements in literacy, life expectancy, and health, and they provided liberal social security coverage. By creating a more informed electorate and a social safety net, the benefits also improved the country's democratic system and helped to ensure social peace. Thirty years after the war, as Marc Edelman notes, "the basic principles of the social welfare state were almost universally accepted."[11]

Costa Rica was able to afford costly education and social programs partly because of increased economic prosperity during the second half of the twentieth century. World demand for coffee and bananas increased in the 1950s and 1960s, along with prices, resulting in new earnings for the country. In addition to paying for social programs, Figueres and other PLN leaders sought to use these earnings to implement a government-controlled industrialization program in Costa Rica. They believed it was important for the government to promote new industries in order to create export products other than coffee and bananas and to protect the economy against downturns in these industries. Their efforts produced successes as well as some failures. One successful example was the creation of a fishing industry, financed entirely by government-owned banks. Tourism also slowly began to earn income for the country during this period. A major investment in beef cattle, however, was largely viewed as a failure. After an initial boom in the 1960s, beef profits fell. Also, cattle ranches produced little employment, damaged large tracts of farmland, and contributed to deforestation. Despite some efforts by the government to promote new industries, however, the country's early prosperity continued to be founded mostly on agricultural exports, which brought in record profits for many years. The resulting prosperity created a large, educated middle class that felt it had a stake in the country's democracy, adding to Costa Rica's political, social, and economic stability.

THE ECONOMIC CRISIS

In the 1970s and 1980s, however, Costa Rica experienced a serious economic crisis that has yet to be fully resolved. The crisis was caused by a variety of factors. One of these was a growing foreign debt that resulted from the government's decision to borrow money from foreign countries in the early years to develop the economy and help pay for its social spending. Adding to this problem was an increasing trade deficit that was caused, in part, by the country's import of large amounts of machinery and other products to support industrialization policies. Furthermore, in 1978 prices for Costa Rica's primary export product, coffee, plummeted, and few other industries existed to pick up the slack. The following year, world oil and fuel prices rose rapidly, and civil wars in neighboring countries interrupted the flow of commerce and caused investors to avoid the region. These economic pressures, in turn, forced the government of President Rodrigo Alberto Carazo Odio (1978–1982) to devalue the colón—Costa Rica's currency—from a high of 8.6 colónes per U.S. dollar in the 1970s to a low of 65 colónes per U.S. dollar in 1982.

By the early 1980s Costa Rica's economy was in real trouble. Inflation had soared to almost 100 percent; industrial production had drastically declined; unemployment had risen to 8.5 percent of the workforce; and a drastic fall in wages had impoverished much of the population. In 1981, with its foreign debt at an alarming $4 billion, Costa Rica was unable to make payments on its loans. Some observers even worried that the deteriorating economic conditions might encourage a military coup and threaten the country's political stability.

Finally, the election in May 1982 of a PLN president, Luis Alberto Monge Álvarez, provided some relief. Ignoring critics' claims that foreign aid might damage Costa Rica's sovereignty, Monge reached out to international institutions for assistance. One such institution was the International Monetary Fund (IMF), an entity that provides loans and financial advice to struggling countries to help them build healthy economies. With IMF loans and advice, Monge was able to restructure Costa Rica's foreign debt, lower inflation, increase economic growth, and bring the country out of the worst of the economic crisis. Also contributing to the country's economic recovery was a dramatic increase in foreign aid from the United States. U.S. aid during the first three years of the Monge administration totaled $643 million, a big jump from the $67 million given by the United States in the previous three-year period (1978-1981).

COSTA RICA'S BANANA INDUSTRY

Bananas have historically been one of Costa Rica's most important agricultural products. Yet the banana industry has often been criticized for creating as many problems as benefits for the country. Banana plantations were first developed in Costa Rica when an American, Minor Cooper Keith, founded the United Fruit Company in Costa Rica in 1888. Keith negotiated to build a railroad in exchange for a grant of large amounts of Costa Rican land in the Caribbean lowlands. United Fruit, however, developed a reputation for paying low wages and providing substandard housing, health care, and food to workers, many of whom were black. In 1934 workers finally organized a large strike that succeeded in garnering government support for workers' rights. In response, United Fruit moved all its operations from the Caribbean area to a remote location on the southern Pacific coast. The government gave in to the industry's refusal to hire former striking workers, passing a law prohibiting former employees from relocating to the Pacific coast. The travel restriction was based on skin color, preventing blacks from traveling beyond the Caribbean region. United Fruit then replicated its low pay and exploitive operations at its new location.

The banana industry has long been vital to Costa Rica's economy. Here, President Figueres shoulders a bunch of the fruit for a photo.

The IMF and other foreign assistance, however, came with conditions. In return for loans, for example, the IMF demanded that the government enact various austerity measures that included increasing exports, diversifying the economy, and slashing government spending. The United States imposed similar conditions and, in addition, expected other types of political and economic cooperation. The austerity conditions demanded from the country have caused cutbacks in Costa Rica's much-beloved education, health, and social systems as well as in hiring by the government, traditionally the nation's primary employer. Austerity programs have also required the sale of inefficient government-owned businesses, demanded major changes in the country's banking and related financial policies and laws, and mandated new income and business taxes. At the same time, the United States and the IMF have pushed Costa Rica to adopt policies of free trade, which seek to abolish tariffs and taxes on imports and exports between countries and promote more worldwide foreign investment and economic competition.

The austerity measures have had some success at diversifying Costa Rica's economy, but at times they have been bitterly protested by workers in Costa Rica. As Wilson explains, many Costa Ricans "feared the economic austerity measures and the accompanying financial cutbacks in social programs would cause a major deterioration of the welfare state."[12] The citizen opposition has forced the government to back down or go much slower on reforms than the international community would like. Noncompliance with international austerity conditions, in turn, has reduced U.S. aid and has held up international loans. Also, because Costa Rica has not yet increased its exports enough to cover its expenses, the country still runs high budget deficits. In addition, the country continues to borrow and pays almost a third of its revenues each year just for the interest on its loans. A full and robust economic recovery, therefore, has yet to be achieved.

COSTA RICA'S GOVERNMENT

Despite the strains of economic turbulence and other problems, Costa Rica continues to be highly respected for its democratic constitution and government. As Richard Biesanz explains, the country "is hailed as admirable and exceptional not only in comparison to most of Latin America, where few countries now hold free elections, but also [throughout much of the less-developed world], where one-party states, dictatorships, and military coups are common."[13]

The current constitution is still largely based on the 1949 constitution, which changed the power balance in Costa Rica to prevent the president from holding too much power. Today's constitution therefore provides for a clear separation of executive, legislative, and judicial powers and for a strong legislature, with numerous checks and balances on presidential power. The executive branch is made up of a president, two vice presidents, and a twelve-member cabinet called the Council of Government. National elections are

held every four years, but a 1969 amendment for many years prohibited the president and legislators from being reelected to consecutive terms (this was overturned finally in 2004). The one-house legislature, called the Legislative Assembly, holds most of the governmental power. It can enact and repeal all laws, impose taxes, approve international agreements, and amend the budget submitted by the president. It is composed of fifty-seven members, who are elected from seven provinces—San José, Alajuela, Cartago, Heredia, Guanacaste, Puntarenas, and Limón. Each province is allotted a specific number of seats in the legislature based on population. A majority vote is required for most measures, but a two-thirds majority is necessary to amend the constitution or override a presidential veto. There is also a highly respected Supreme Court of Justice composed of twenty-two magistrates (judges), whose terms are automatically renewed each year unless the legislature decides to remove them. Lower courts include civil and criminal courts in each of the provinces.

Under the constitution, all citizens eighteen and older are permitted to vote, and there is broad freedom of expression,

U.S. president Ronald Reagan meets with Costa Rican president Luis Alberto Monge Álvarez. Monge solicited millions of dollars in aid from the United States.

assembly, and religion. The Supreme Electoral Tribunal (TSE), the independent body created in 1949 to oversee elections and ensure that they are peaceful, continues to perform an essential role. It acts as a watchdog over all aspects of elections, including voter registration, political campaigns, electoral laws, and voting procedures. It also provides funding to political candidates and regulates citizenship issues. The TSE is made up of three magistrates who are appointed by the Supreme Court for six-year terms.

In addition, consistent with Costa Rica's preference for avoiding concentrations of power, there are numerous ministries charged with various government functions. These institutions are given great freedom and independence, and each has its own budget and staff. These include, to name just a few, the Ministry of Economy, Industry, and Commerce; the Ministry of Environment and Energy; the Ministry of Health; the Ministry of Finance; the Ministry of Public Education; the Ministry of Interior and Police; and the Ministry of Science and Technology. There is also a National Institute for Women and a Costa Rican Institute on Tourism,

An elderly man in a retirement home casts his vote during the presidential election of 2002. Voting is a constitutional right extended to all Costa Ricans over the age of eighteen.

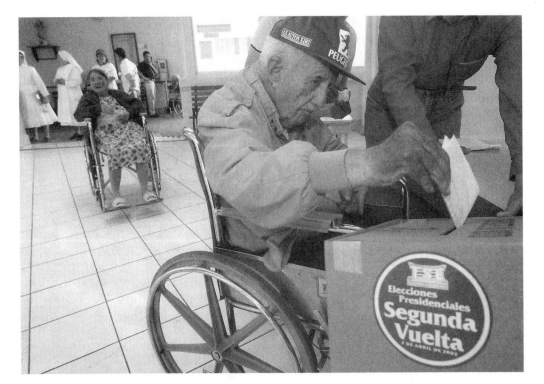

along with many other commissions and institutions. There is no army, navy, or air force, however. Since 1949, when Figueres disbanded the military, Costa Rica has had only a police force. In addition to normal civil policing duties, this force has a military capability and is charged with policing the country's borders.

Costa Rica's government system has produced two main political parties, the PLN and an opposition party that often changes with each election. Founded in 1951 by José Figueres, the PLN for most of the years since then has held a majority in the legislature, even when the elected president was not a PLN candidate. The PLN's opposition has usually been a coalition that gets pulled together to back a candidate just before each election. In recent years the strongest opposition party has been the Social Christian Unity Party (PUSC). Various minor third parties also often win seats in the legislature, but none has ever won a campaign for the presidency.

Most Costa Ricans regard democracy as a great treasure to be protected. Citizens are automatically issued election identification cards on their eighteenth birthdays, and voting is mandatory (although the failure to vote is not punished). Election Day, held the first Sunday in February every fourth year, is a public holiday, and the great majority of Costa Ricans gaily visit the polls to cast their votes amid honking cars and flying confetti. As travel writer Paul Theroux has said, elections in Costa Rica are "something of a fiesta."[14] After each election, however, power peacefully transfers to the new leaders, historically without allegations of voter fraud, and people go about their normal business. Each election since the 1940s has thus confirmed the country's long tradition of peaceful and fair democracy.

POLITICAL TRENDS

Modern elections in Costa Rica have largely been dominated by economic issues and have seen both PLN and opposition candidates elected. In 1986, following PLN president Monge's term, another PLN candidate, Oscar Arias Sánchez, was elected president to carry on Monge's economic reforms. He helped revive and diversify the economy by promoting tourism and nontraditional exports, such as exotic flowers and fruits, and helped to decrease the country's dependence

President Oscar Arias's Peace Plan

Costa Rican president Oscar Arias made news around the world in 1987 when he negotiated a plan to bring peace to the troubled nations of Central America. In August 1987 Arias was successful in finalizing a peace agreement among five Central American countries that ended Nicaragua's civil war and other regional conflicts and won Arias the 1987 Nobel Peace Prize. In a speech to the U.S. Congress on September 22, 1987, reprinted in *The Costa Rica Reader*, a collection of materials edited by Marc Edelman and Joanne Kenen, Arias explained:

The peace plan encourages national reconciliation in countries where brothers are set against brothers. . . . We ask for dialogue and amnesty, a cease-fire as soon as possible, and democratization without delay. We call for elections reflecting the true will of the majority of the people. We call for the suspension of military aid to insurgencies. We want guarantees that no territories will be used to attack other states. . . . In an atmosphere of democracy and freedom, we can return to the path of development that will enable a lasting peace.

Oscar Arias won the Nobel Peace Prize in 1987 for his plan to end the civil war in Nicaragua.

on coffee and bananas. He also signed a trade agreement with Mexico, reducing trade tariffs between the two countries.

President Arias, however, was also confronted with a foreign policy dilemma—the possibility of a regional war that could have threatened the country's dedication to peace and neutrality. The threat came from the neighboring countries of Nicaragua, El Salvador, and Guatemala, each of which was grappling with destabilizing civil conflicts. Nicaragua, especially, had been a threat to Costa Rica for decades. Nicaragua's president, General Anastasio Somoza, had been an enemy of Costa Rican leader José Figueres since the 1940s, when Somoza sent Nicaraguan troops into Costa Rica during its civil war. Afterwards, the two countries took widely diverging paths: Costa Rica chose disarmament and democracy, while Nicaragua, under the Somoza family, became a militarized dictatorship. The years of repression in Nicaragua produced an opposition force of fighters called the Sandinistas, who, in 1979, staged a revolution and took over the Nicaraguan government, toppling Somoza. Costa Ricans cheered this development, but later Costa Rican president Monge was pressured by the United States to allow anti-Sandinista fighters, called Contras, to establish bases in Costa Rica and conduct raids into Nicaragua. This placed Costa Rica in the dangerous position of helping to overthrow a neighboring country's government—a role that violated Costa Rica's historical claim to peace and neutrality toward such military entanglements. The Nicaraguan conflict, along with similar military conflicts in other Central American countries, also brought thousands of refugees into Costa Rica and

A group of Contra forces sails down the San Juan River in Nicaragua in 1983. The United States supported the Contras in their fight against the Sandinistas in Nicaragua.

PRESIDENT ABEL PACHECO DE LA ESPRIELLA

On May 5, 2002, Abel Pacheco de la Espriella was inaugurated as Costa Rica's president. Pacheco was born in 1933 in San José, the son of a banana farmer. He studied medicine and psychiatry, was a commentator on Costa Rican television, taught at the University of Costa Rica, and ran a clothing business in downtown San José. He also wrote several novels and a number of popular songs. In 1988 Pacheco began his political career when he was elected to Costa Rica's legislature to represent San José.

In his 2002 presidential inaugural speech, Pacheco proposed an ambitious agenda. In addition to a war on poverty, he proposed that environmental protections be made part of the nation's constitution. Pacheco also promised to improve the country's ports, airports, and the road network and to modernize energy services, telecommunications, and the Internet. At the same time, Pacheco promised to continue past economic policies by pushing for privatization of state-owned businesses and by negotiating free-trade treaties with the United States and other countries. Pacheco succeeded in negotiating free-trade agreements, but he has faced difficulties fulfilling many of his other promises due to economic difficulties, bureaucratic obstacles, and citizen opposition.

President Abel Pacheco (right) meets with two U.S. senators in 2004 to discuss the free-trade agreement.

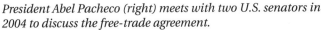

hurt the country's economy by preventing foreign investment in the region.

Outraged at U.S. actions that drew Costa Rica into a war against Nicaragua and interested in finding a way to end the regional conflicts, President Arias resisted U.S. pressure to support the Contras. Instead, Arias called for U.S. cooperation in seeking a negotiated settlement to the conflict in Nicaragua and presented the presidents of Guatemala, El Salvador, and Honduras with a formal peace proposal to end all regional fighting. Later peace talks included Nicaragua. Finally, in August 1987, all five Central American countries signed a peace plan that brought an end to hostilities in Central America. The plan called for cease-fires for all the regional conflicts, the end of U.S. and other outside military aid to antigovernment forces, amnesty for political prisoners, free elections, and negotiations between governments and opposition groups. Arias won the Nobel Peace Prize in 1987 for his efforts and has remained highly popular among Costa Ricans.

With the Nicaragua issue resolved, economic issues again dominated politics in the 1990s. Rafael Ángel Calderón Fournier, son of the former president, was elected president in 1990 as the opposition party candidate. Under pressure from the IMF, he privatized government-owned businesses, further decreased state spending on social welfare, and imposed new taxes. Control of the government again shifted from the opposition to the PLN in 1994, when José María Figueres Olsen, son of President José Figueres Ferrer, was elected as the PLN candidate. Figueres, however, was forced by international and economic pressures to follow this same path of privatizing state businesses. He also encouraged new industries and foreign investment and embraced the worldwide trend toward free trade. For example, in 1997 Figueres convinced Intel, a giant computer chip manufacturer, to build a large assembly plant in Costa Rica. This and other similar investments have helped the country to bring in more manufacturing income. The next president, opposition candidate Miguel Ángel Rodriguez Echeverría (1998–2002), tried to continue privatization of state industries, such as electric utilities, but he was stopped by large-scale protests staged by citizens who feared loss of jobs and higher utility prices. He did, however, sign free-trade deals with Mexico and Canada.

In 2002 another opposition party candidate, Abel Pacheco de la Espriella, was elected with limited voter support based on promises to continue economic reforms, to create jobs, and to end poverty. Pacheco has had difficulty implementing these policies, due to a slow economy, strikes by government workers protesting privatization, and other problems. In 2004, however, Pacheco signed free-trade agreements with both the United States and CARICOM, a trade alliance of Caribbean countries.

The trend in Costa Rica's government therefore appears to be a continuation of Costa Ricans' historical tendency toward switching and distributing power among different parties in order to avoid concentrations of power that might be dangerous to democracy. In addition, Costa Ricans have strongly supported peace negotiations and have fought to preserve the social welfare system, forcing their leaders to implement economic austerity measures incrementally and to spread the pain of budget cuts broadly across the population. Through all their many modern challenges, therefore, Costa Ricans have tried to remain true to their core values of protecting their democracy, providing liberal social benefits, and promoting peace.

Costa Rican Society

Contributing to Costa Rica's political and social stability is a highly homogeneous culture that has experienced little ethnic or other social conflict. Instead, Costa Rican society is largely marked by strong national pride, hospitality and civility, and strong family values. Some ethnic discrimination is evident, but whatever social divisions exist are increasingly based largely on class or wealth differences.

Tico Society

Costa Ricans call themselves "Ticos" (or for females, "Ticas"). As Christopher P. Baker explains, these terms come from a colonial saying—"we are all *hermaniticos* (little brothers)."[15] Ticos are extremely proud of their country and think of themselves as Costa Ricans rather than as Central Americans. Although this sometimes causes resentment among people in neighboring countries, it is largely a reflection of a positive value—Costa Ricans' strong love for their country and their understandable appreciation for the policies of peace, literacy, and democracy that have characterized their recent political history.

Ticos' sense of pride also reflects certain inherent cultural values, such as optimism, modesty, industriousness, and personal humility. Costa Ricans, for example, are known for their cheerfulness, humor, friendliness, and politeness. Indeed, visitors to Costa Rica often note that Costa Ricans are an exceedingly warm and hospitable people, eager to get along with others. Also, they seem always to be trying to make a positive impression; as a result, they try to avoid gossip, dress, or behavior that could reflect badly on themselves. As professor Charlene Helmuth describes, "People are careful to always look their best, with pants pressed and shoes shined, fully made up, or wearing jewelry. It is not uncommon to see women in high heels even at the grocery store."[16]

One explanation for this strong cultural identity is that Costa Rican society developed into a highly homogeneous

Because most Costa Ricans like these are lighter-skinned than other Latin Americans, Ticos generally consider themselves "white" rather than "Hispanic."

one in which there are few social divisions. During the colonial period, Europeans from Spain quickly outnumbered the small groups of surviving indigenous people (sometimes called Indians), many of whom intermarried with the Spanish settlers. This created a society comprised largely of whites and light-skinned mestizos (descendants of predominantly Spanish and some Indian ancestry). The majority of Costa Ricans today are part of this mestizo society, but they tend to be lighter-skinned than mestizos from neighboring countries, and they call themselves "white" rather than "Hispanic." As Baker has noted, "The vast majority of Costa Ricans look predominantly European."[17] They speak primarily Spanish and often some English.

This majority makes up 94 percent of the country's total population. The rest of Costa Rica's population is made up of several small ethnic groups, including native inhabitants, blacks, and Chinese minorities. The overwhelming size of the white and mestizo majority group compared to the tiny numbers of minorities, experts say, largely accounts for the absence of significant racial or ethnic conflict in Costa Rica.

ETHNIC MINORITIES

One of the minority groups in Costa Rica is made up of descendants of various indigenous tribes. They are sometimes called Indians, but they prefer to be called *indígenas* (meaning "native inhabitants"). Today, a total of about thirty thousand *indígenas* live in Costa Rica, forming only about 1 percent of the total population. They belong to six different linguistic groups, and although an increasing number also speak Spanish, many still speak their native languages. Most *indígenas* live on twenty-two Indian reserves created by the government in 1977 near the southern border and farther north on the Pacific coast. There, they remain isolated from the rest of Costa Rican society. Today, *indígena* lands, however, are threatened by development as ranchers, farmers, and mining companies seek to buy up or seize native lands for their commercial purposes. *Indígenas* also suffer from government neglect. The government now funds programs to promote their language and culture, but over the years *indígenas* have often been given inferior education, health, and social services compared to the majority population. Furthermore, *indígenas* have only been allowed to vote since 1994.

TYPICAL TICO EXPRESSIONS

Although the majority of Costa Ricans speak Spanish like much of the rest of Central America, they are known for their unique speech patterns and sayings. Costa Ricans tend to soften and slur their *r*'s so that the *r* sound is pronounced almost as a whistle. In addition, Ticos are famous for using the diminutive ending, *-tico*. For example, *chiquito* (meaning "very little") might be changed to *chiquitico* (meaning "little bitty"). Ticos also have numerous popular expressions. One is *pura vida* (meaning "pure life"), which is a typical response to the question "What's going on." This saying reflects typical Costa Rican optimism and means that life is good. Other expressions reflect Costa Ricans' love of humor. Examples include *más serio que un burro en lancha* (a criticism that means "more serious than a donkey in a rowboat") and *por donde pasa la suegra* (a description of light housekeeping that means "where the mother-in-law might pass by"—referring to places where the mother-in-law might easily see dust or dirt).

Costa Rica also has a small black minority numbering around one hundred thousand, or about 3 percent of the population. A few of these black Costa Ricans are descended from Caribbean immigrants who traveled to Limón as early as 1825 and stayed to work as fishermen and farmers. Most of the country's blacks, however, are descendents from Jamaica, part of the British West Indies, who were brought to Costa Rica during the late nineteenth century to work on Costa Rica's humid Caribbean coast building the country's first railroad. After the railroad was built, most found work on east coast banana plantations. When banana companies moved their operations to the Pacific side of Costa Rica in the 1930s, many blacks started their own small subsistence farms growing bananas and cacao. Rising cacao prices in the mid-1950s allowed many of these black landowners to rise out of poverty.

Today, many blacks continue to live in southeastern Costa Rica. They speak a colorful Creole type of English, and the majority work as farmers and dockworkers or in government jobs. Yet observers agree that there is discrimination against blacks. As Richard Biesanz explains, "The idea that blacks are not really Ticos is often stated or implied. Many white Costa Ricans think of blacks as stupid or ugly, and consider them good only for sports, music, and work."[18] Although recognized as citizens and awarded voting rights by the government in 1949, blacks often received poor education and were segregated from much of the country's political, economic, and social life. Today, this racism persists, but blacks are increasingly acquiring better education, and some are moving to San José or to other countries to seek better opportunities.

Yet another tiny ethnic group, composing about 1 percent of the population, is made up of descendants of six hundred Chinese laborers brought to Costa Rica in 1873 to help build the railroad. The Chinese immigrants were paid only one-fifth of the normal wage, had to endure terrible living and working conditions, and were expected to be sent home as soon as the work was completed. After the railroad was built, however, many Chinese were sold to wealthy Costa Ricans to work as household servants. Today, their descendants live throughout the country and own most of the retail stores and other establishments in the lowland areas. Others work in agricultural jobs near Limón. Although older Chinese of-

ten segregated themselves away from Tico society, many younger Chinese have blended into the larger community.

This photo captures a typical afternoon scene on a veranda in front of a shop in the Caribbean town of Cahuita, whose population is predominately black.

CLASS DIFFERENCES AND STANDARDS OF LIVING

Despite the clear evidence of discrimination that has disadvantaged some ethnic groups, Ticos like to believe that Costa Rica is a classless society in which everyone is treated with respect and dignity regardless of their wealth or status. This myth arose during colonial times, when much of Costa Rica's society was made up of many small farms, and these farmers had relatively close relations with other, poorer members of the community. This society stood in stark contrast to many other Spanish colonies in Central America, in which just a few very large, wealthy landowners separated themselves from and reigned over a large number of very poor indigenous peasants. As Biesanz explains, "Because there were few Indians to conquer or enslave and little gold or silver to exploit, [an aristocracy] . . . could not arise in colonial Costa Rica. Extremes of wealth and poverty were [therefore] far less pronounced and land far more evenly distributed than in most other colonies."[19] This belief in the fairness of Costa

LATIN REFUGEES IN COSTA RICA

In recent decades Costa Rica increasingly has attracted refugees, mostly Hispanics from neighboring Central American countries that were experiencing civil wars and political turmoil. During the 1970s, for example, up to 100,000 Nicaraguans crossed the border while fleeing that government's terror tactics. Many of these refugees returned to Nicaragua after the Sandinista party's victory in 1979. Soon, however, these immigrants were replaced by refugees fleeing violence in El Salvador and later by more Nicaraguans after insurgents began a war against the Sandinista government. By 1989, 43,000 documented refugees were living in Costa Rica. After peace was achieved in Central America, however, there was not as great a refugee flow. Today, Costa Rican law still provides for granting refugee status or asylum to eligible persons, and the refugee population numbers about 14,000, including 8,760 refugees escaping recent violent uprisings in Colombia. However, many more immigrants now travel to Costa Rica for economic rather than political reasons. They seek work and often are hired illegally on farms and are paid very low wages. Although once more warmly embraced, immigrants now are seen more as a burden, and they sometimes face open discrimination in Tico society.

Rican society gained more popularity as a result of the country's broad program of education and social reforms, which lifted many Costa Ricans into middle-class status.

Experts agree, however, that class differences do exist in the country. Even in colonial Costa Rica, the colonists were divided into hidalgos (nobles) and *plebeyos* (common people). Hidalgos were granted many special rights by the Spanish government. Only they could serve in local government councils, and they controlled the land and often owned slaves. The poverty of the Costa Rican settlement blurred some of these distinctions, and hidalgos intermarried with some indigenous people, but a small group of elite hidalgo families continued to hold most of the political and economic power. After independence, these elites retained their hold largely by taking control of the growing coffee trade. Thereafter, they dominated Costa Rica's government for many decades. President Guardia's policies and the country's embrace of meaningful social reforms curbed some of the power of the elites and gave many Costa Ricans the chance to improve their economic and social status, but class distinctions have never been completely erased.

Today in Costa Rica there is still a small elite, most of whom are descendants of the original hidalgo families from colonial times. Although they compose only about 5 percent of the population, they control a large part of the country's economy and receive as much as one-quarter of the country's total income. Below them is a sizable middle class made up of some self-made and newly rich people who have no hidalgo family connections, a number of well-off professionals, and a broad contingent of lower-paid Ticos who work as teachers, nurses, and small farmers or business owners. At the very bottom of society is a group of poor Costa Ricans who work in manual or unskilled jobs. This group includes both unskilled urban workers, who work in jobs such as janitors, gardeners, and domestic workers, and poor rural peasants, who work in agriculture or other laborer jobs. The country's recent economic problems have also resulted in greater poverty and a growing population of unemployed.

FAMILY AND TRADITION
Regardless of wealth or class status, tradition and conservative values still play an important role throughout the dominant Tico culture. Family, in particular, remains a central

Poor, unskilled laborers like these coffee pickers in San José occupy the bottom rung of Costa Rican society.

WOMEN IN COSTA RICAN SOCIETY

Women in Costa Rica can point to many advancements, but they still face many obstacles to equality in their society. On the positive side, women along with men have been provided access to education and health care, giving them the same high rates of literacy and life expectancy. Costa Rican women also receive free hospitalization for childbirth as well as mandatory maternity leave. Women were granted the right to vote in 1949, and laws on divorce and property rights are favorable to women. In 1990 the country passed the Bill for Women's True Equality, which, among other reforms, eliminated sexist content from teaching materials. Costa Rica's legal system has also been revised to provide protections against domestic violence. Other advancements include the election of many more women into political office and the rise of women in government, medical, and legal fields. Yet attitudes of "machismo," common in Latin cultures,

still exist in Costa Rica. These attitudes give more social freedoms to males and create inequalities and discrimination for women in the workplace. Women earn less than men, and most positions of power and prestige in Costa Rica continue to be held by males.

Although many Costa Rican women like this doctor are employed in advanced professions, women still face many prejudices in everyday life.

part of society and leisure activities. Indeed, despite the apparent friendliness of Ticos, closer relationships are often limited to family and just a few long-term friends. As Baker explains, "Family bonds are so strong that foreigners often find making intimate relationships a challenge."[20] Many young girls still aspire toward marriage and children, and many marry when they are still quite young, typically before age twenty-five. Although declining birth rates have made large families no longer as common as in the past, one or two children are welcomed and doted on, and their health and education are considered the highest of parents' priorities.

Costa Ricans' tendency toward tradition can also be seen in the measure of formality they attach to social behaviors. For example, social interactions follow a ritual of formally greeting everyone in the room and saying goodbye when leaving, and Ticos go out of their way to be courteous, complimentary, and to avoid offending others in conversation. Sometimes this means stretching the truth to say things they do not mean. For example, Ticos are famous for promising to do something *mañana* (tomorrow), but often this simply means they will not keep the promise at all.

This formality and tradition also extends to dating activities and marriage rituals. Most single Costa Ricans live at home and socialize in groups until a formal dating ritual begins. Once dating begins, many families still expect the man to "court" the woman through chaperoned visits to the woman's home. Sex is expected to be postponed until after marriage. Eventually, the man asks the father for the woman's hand in marriage and the two are married, usually in a traditional Catholic ceremony. After marriage, the pair might even live with parents or other family members, an extended family system that has the advantage of providing help to aging relatives. Traditionally, divorce is frowned upon and pressure is placed on couples to stay together. These traditional ideals are still valued and followed by some families in Costa Rica.

Recent societal changes, however, have eroded many traditional values. For many young people, dating now often takes place before the man is introduced to the woman's family, and many more couples have sex before marriage and consider divorce an option if the relationship does not work out. More couples also form unions, and have children together, without getting married, and children are sometimes born as a result of married men having affairs with single women. Because of these types of changes, Costa Rica has seen an increase in one-parent (often female-headed) families, particularly among the poor. In fact, a large number of households are now matriarchal families, in which a grandmother, a working daughter, and the daughter's children live together without a man. In addition, Costa Rica has seen increases in the number of singles and older adults living alone, and some people even show an acceptance of gay lifestyles. Other signs of societal changes include more drunkenness and crimes such as theft, fraud, and burglary. The use and trading of illegal drugs are also on the rise. In fact, parts of Costa Rica, such as Limón, have been identified by the U.S. Drug Enforcement Agency as critical drug-trade areas.

RELIGION

Despite the recent changes in society, the overwhelming majority of Costa Ricans still ascribe to the Roman Catholic religion. Historically, the church functioned as one of the country's most powerful institutions, second only to the government, and it played an active and important role in the country's early development. The first Catholic church, for example, was founded by Spanish settlers in Costa Rica at Cartago, and Catholic missionaries quickly converted the indigenous population, making Catholicism the only accepted religion both in the colony and after independence. In the 1940s the Catholic Church actively supported the social reforms sought by the Calderón government. Later, church leaders backed PLN leaders such as Presidents Monge and Arias as they tried to address the country's economic problems without destroying the social welfare system.

Today, however, the Catholic Church's influence on Costa Ricans has weakened. Although still important to mark baptisms, deaths, and marriages, the Catholic religion is less important to people's daily lives than in the past. The majority of Costa Rican Roman Catholics do not even attend mass regularly. Catholic churches, however, still form the symbolic center of almost every town and city, religious holidays dominate the calendar, and popular speech often includes references to saints and religious symbols. As Charlene Helmuth notes, "The influence of Catholic traditions runs deep, and the Church provides a significant social network that is the heart of virtually every community."[21]

At the same time, some Costa Ricans have been drawn to evangelical Protestant churches, such as those of the Assemblies of God, Seventh-Day Adventists, Church of the

Catholics take part in a Good Friday procession through the streets of Limón. The church is the symbolic core of Costa Rican life.

Nazarene, Mennonites, and Fundamentalist Baptists. These various evangelical churches first became popular among the West Indian black population on the Caribbean coast and have spread since the 1960s to encompass other segments of the country's population. Now, more than 16 percent of the population follows these evangelical faiths. Many of these churches were founded by U.S. missionaries who traveled to Costa Rica in the 1960s and 1970s.

Besides this evangelical movement, a few Costa Ricans also follow other religions, including Protestant denominations such as Methodism and Anglicanism, Judaism, Buddhism, Hinduism, the Church of Latter-day Saints, and Jehovah's Witnesses.

EDUCATION, HEALTH, AND HOUSING

Another important value to Costa Ricans is education, an issue on which the government has historically placed great emphasis. Education was the cornerstone of the country's social reforms during the 1940s. Since then, it has become one of the primary responsibilities of the government. As

Helmuth notes, "For 50 years, the government has devoted a significant portion—nearly 30 percent—of its budget to education."[22] These expenditures resulted in a 96 percent literacy rate, the highest in Central America, and helped many Costa Ricans and their children to live more prosperous lives.

Today, education is still highly revered in Costa Rica. In 1992 the government declared education to be a fundamental right of every citizen. School is free for grades one through twelve and compulsory between the ages of six and fifteen. The government also provides funding to needy students for higher education at public universities, including the University of Costa Rica, the country's largest university, and several other public colleges and technical schools. In fact, more than seventy thousand students are enrolled at these public institutions. In return for this free education, students at public schools and universities are required to donate time toward community service after they graduate. Citizen support for these education programs is so strong that when budget cuts were proposed as a result of the country's economic problems, students and others protested, preventing many of the proposed cuts. Yet there have been funding and program changes that many believe have resulted in a reduction in the quality of teachers and education. In re-

Students at a school in the town of Tortuguero line up for an outdoor assembly. The social reforms of the 1940s targeted education as a priority.

sponse, numerous private schools have been established in Costa Rica in recent years. These are attended by those who can afford them—mostly students from middle or upper classes. The wealthy also often send their children abroad to study.

Yet another part of the social security system that was started during the 1940s in Costa Rica is a health system that rivals that of many larger and wealthier countries. As San José journalist Isabel de Bertodano notes, "In 2001 the World Health Organization ranked the small Central American nation of Costa Rica 36th out of 191 countries for health system performance."[23] Today, 89 percent of Costa Ricans are covered by the national health care program, which provides high-quality, localized, preventative, and primary health care. Despite budget constraints, the system has been modernized in recent years to improve efficiency, provide better services, and make local providers more accountable for monies spent. Over the years, these health services have greatly improved health, reduced malnutrition, and increased life expectancy, and even poor rural Costa Ricans now can count on being treated if they become ill.

The country's social security net, however, has not been extended to equalize housing conditions. The quality of housing today, as in the past, varies widely according to class status. Wealthier Costa Ricans typically live in large, gated houses, with manicured lawns, outdoor courtyards or patios, and garages. These are usually located on wide, paved, and neatly kept streets in urban areas such as San José and surrounding cities. The houses of poorer urban residents, in contrast, are smaller and more run-down, with fewer luxuries and not as many rooms. Many of the poorest people live in urban slums, where dwellings often consist of makeshift shacks or crowded apartment buildings. In more rural areas, the poor may live in even less adequate housing. Some rural shanties may consist of one or two rooms and a dirt or wooden-plank floor, although most now have electricity and running water.

Although there is still much to do to lift up the lives of some in Costa Rica, the country remains much more stable and peaceful than other areas of Central America, and it can be proud that its largely harmonious society rivals that of other countries around the world.

5

Arts and Leisure

Decades of peace, democracy, and relative prosperity, combined with beautiful natural surroundings and great weather, have encouraged Costa Ricans to value their leisure time. These conditions have also produced a vibrant social, music, media, and arts scene in the country. Today, Costa Rica is a lively and stimulating place, both for the country's residents and its many tourists.

Traditional Leisure Activities

Costa Ricans are known for their love of leisure and relaxed lifestyles. Most citizens work or go to school, but often schedules are short, with long lunches and a five-day workweek, leaving ample time for play in the evenings and on weekends. The mild weather and beautiful natural surroundings further encourage relaxation and fun, and Costa Ricans do not feel guilty about enjoying their lives. Ticos, in fact, have a common expression for aimless relaxation, *matando la culebra* ("killing the snake"); it is derived from the explanation banana plantation workers used to give their bosses when asked what they had been doing in the jungle instead of working.

Traditionally, Costa Ricans spent most of their free time with family and neighbors, chatting and telling stories or jokes after meals. Wealthier landowners often visited each other's homes for games, poetry recitals, dances, or singing, or they rode into the countryside for daytime picnics. Working-class men, on the other hand, have long enjoyed gathering after work at the local pool hall, the *pulpería*, to drink and mingle with their friends. Women traditionally satisfied their social needs by visiting with family or friends and attending church, local church fairs, or town fiestas (festivals). For everyone, the local coffee harvest was a time of celebration, when people could socialize and flirt.

Today, Costa Ricans still spend a great deal of time with family. Weekend activities for many families often include

Sunday visits to a wide circle of relatives or attendance at various family weddings, funerals, and other events. Also, as Charlene Helmuth explains, "Family members are much more likely to be automatically involved in birthdays, holidays, ceremonies, even vacations, than they would in the United States."[24] The *pulpería*, too, continues to be popular in rural areas, providing liquor, pool tables, and television for male patrons. In cities, more upscale bars and cocktail

A family enjoys a motorcycle ride. Ticos treasure their free time, which usually involves spending time with family.

lounges offer similar companionship opportunities for men. Women often meet close friends or professional colleagues in their homes or for lunches or other outings. As in other developed societies, however, Costa Ricans also have plenty of other leisure activities from which to choose.

HOLIDAYS AND FIESTAS

Costa Ricans especially love celebrations, and they turn out in large numbers for numerous fiestas held to mark important holidays, honor a town's patron saint, or raise money for local causes. Indeed, the country's calendar includes so many holidays that government and business leaders have sought to limit their number. The most important holidays in Costa Rica, however, continue to be Independence Day (September 15), San José Day (December 28), New Year's Day (January 1), and religious holidays such as Christmas and Easter. For these major holidays, businesses, schools, and stores are closed and a carnival atmosphere prevails, sometimes with parades or public ceremonies, and often with fireworks set off to mark the occasion. Families and friends typically gather together in homes for meals and visits or head off on day trips to the beach or the mountains. Christmas and Easter are celebrated in similar ways, but with more emphasis on food and religious traditions.

For Christmas, for example, most Costa Ricans decorate their homes with lights and a Christian nativity scene, and they prepare traditional holiday foods, including grapes, apples, and tamales—a delicious combination of cornmeal and chicken or pork, with rice, olives, raisins, and seasonings, wrapped in banana leaves. Costa Ricans also spend weeks shopping for Christmas gifts, and they send greeting cards to all their friends and business associates. On Christmas Eve, families celebrate by eating, drinking, dancing, and socializing. At midnight, they place the Christ child into the nativity scene, and attend midnight mass. Often the merrymaking then continues until dawn, when the children get up and open the Christmas presents brought by Santa Claus.

Easter, celebrated for a full week, brings another excuse to party. Although celebrated more as a religious holiday than Christmas, especially in more rural parts of the country, Easter nevertheless is also another vacation from work and school and a chance to relax and socialize with family and friends.

In addition to these national holidays, Costa Ricans attend numerous local fairs and fiestas held throughout the year. Annual fiestas, for example, are held in most cities and towns to honor patron saints, and other street fairs are organized at various times to raise money for schools or churches. These often elaborate celebrations are planned long in advance by local volunteers, and they feature an array of foods, music, and activities. Women prepare tamales, beef stew, and other popular dishes, and local bands play music. Fireworks, soccer games, clowns, dancing, and beauty pageants are other typical fiesta highlights. Gambling is also popular in Costa Rica, and fiestas often run raffles or lotteries to raise money.

MUSIC AND DANCE

Holidays and fiestas are always occasions for music and dance, which are enjoyed by all Costa Ricans, but particularly by teenagers and young adults. Music and dancing are also quite popular at private parties, schools, and at both small-town dance halls and larger city nightclubs and bars. Nightclubs, in fact, are one of the favorite hangouts for young people. On most nights and weekends, clubs in urban areas such as San José are usually packed and their dance floors are crowded with romantic couples. As Chrisopher P. Baker describes, "Ticos

Schoolgirls march in a 2003 Independence Day parade. Ticos turn out in large numbers to celebrate their country's many holidays.

love to dance . . . [their] celebrated reserve gives way to outrageously flirtatious dancing befitting a land of passionate men and women."[25]

At the dance clubs and discos, traditional Latin dance music styles, such as salsa, *cumbia*, *lambada*, and *meringue*, are

COSTA RICA'S COWBOYS

Costa Rica's northwestern province of Guanacaste is the site of vast stretches of savannahs (grasslands). The region is home to numerous large cattle ranches that employ Costa Rica's version of cowboys, called *sabaneros*. The *sabaneros* work the cattle, take care of the horses, and perform all the various chores necessary on these working cattle ranches. In this region of plains and rolling hills, there is virtually no rain during the dry season and less rain than elsewhere in the country even during the rainy season. In many ways, therefore, the area is comparable to parts of California and has been called Costa Rica's Wild West. Life here revolves around horses and cattle ranching, and the ranches produce the majority of the country's beef products. For entertainment, *sabaneros* compete in rodeos and bullfights, and they participate in the region's colorful horse parades, which show off their beautiful and well-groomed horses along with their impressive riding skills. Tourists to this colorful area can rent horses for horseback rides into the countryside or even spend a day working alongside a ranch's *sabaneros*.

A sabanero *holds on as he rides a bucking horse at a rodeo in the province of Guanacaste, home to many cattle ranches.*

the most common. These music styles produce a strong, almost hypnotic beat mixed with intriguing rhythms that are infectious for dancing. Other popular musical styles in Costa Rica include U.S. rock and pop tunes as well as calypso, a type of Afro-Caribbean music from Costa Rica's Caribbean coast. Calypso combines African music, Spanish influences, and American jazz and rhythm and blues.

Other musical styles of Costa Rica also have African or Spanish roots. Folk music often features the marimba, or xylophone, an African percussion instrument made of wood that produces a mellow and melodious sound. The Spanish guitar, too, is a popular instrument. It often accompanies folk dances such as the *Punto Guanacaste*, a traditional couples dance often performed by folk dance groups who tour the country and perform at national venues. Costa Rica also has symphony and chamber orchestras that play various forms of classical music. The National Symphony Orchestra, for example, was given strong government support beginning in the 1970s. Today, it is widely respected and has toured in the United States, Europe, and other countries.

SPORTS
In addition to dancing, Costa Ricans enjoy other physical activities. Given the weather and environment, most Costa Ricans are accustomed to regular physical exercise and outdoor activities. They are used to walking everywhere to shop or socialize, even in cities where there are public transportation systems. Outdoor water and ecological activities such as bird-watching, hiking, fishing, yachting, scuba diving, whitewater rafting, and surfing are also increasingly catching on with tourists as well as locals.

Organized sports, too, have long been quite popular. Swimming, soccer, and cycling are probably the most-loved sports, but others, such as basketball, volleyball, boxing, wrestling, tennis, golf, and running, have their followings as well. These sports are played in schools, public parks, and private clubs. In addition, Costa Rica has sponsored various national teams that have won Olympic and other international tournaments. In the 1996 Olympics, for example, Costa Rican Claudia Poll set a world record and won a gold medal for the two hundred-meter freestyle swim. Equestrian events, too, have a long tradition in the country, especially in the northwestern cattle-ranching area of Guanacaste province, where cowboys compete in colorful rodeo competitions.

By far the most important sport to Costa Ricans, however, is soccer. Most young working-class males spend much of their free time kicking around a soccer ball and perfecting their skills. Virtually every city and town, no matter how small, sponsors at least one soccer team, and competitions at various levels are held around the country almost every Sunday. The soccer games attract large crowds of both male and female spectators, who watch and cheer with great spirit and emotion. For national games, crowds of thirty thousand are not uncommon.

TRAVEL AND FOOD
Costa Ricans also love to travel, both inside and outside the country. Those who can afford it travel abroad regularly, especially to the United States and Europe. Many people also travel within Costa Rica, exploring its varied geography, attractions, and resorts. Indeed, the government has sponsored campaigns to encourage domestic travel and enhance the great pride Costa Ricans have in their country. Favorite destinations include the many beautiful beaches and resorts that line both the Caribbean and Pacific coasts, the rugged inland mountains, and the numerous national parks that offer the chance to appreciate the country's spectacular flora and fauna.

Often, too, families will just pile into a car during the weekend to find a new place to eat. As Helmuth describes, "Costa Ricans take great pride in their country and its regional distinctions, [and] they seek out contact with, and the experience of, what they perceive as their 'authentic culture.'"[26] The country's various provinces and regions, for example, each have their own food specialties, which often attract travelers. One such cultural specialty in San Ramón is *cajeta*, a sweet confection made from creamy milk. Other regional fare includes seafood in Puntarenas, corn dishes in Guanacaste, and Caribbean-style coconut-milk dishes in Limón.

The staple cuisine of Costa Rica, however, is rice, black beans, and corn tortillas, accompanied by vegetables or a salad. Typically, the food is not spicy but is flavored with

herbs such as cilantro and fresh, sweet red peppers. Indeed, Costa Rican cooking is known for its use of a wide variety of garden fresh fruits and vegetables, which can be purchased at small local markets or at weekly farmers' markets.

Yet Ticos also enjoy finer dining. Typical dishes include the national dish, a meat stew called *olla de carne*, made from squash, corn, potatoes, tubers such as yucca, green plantains, and beef. Another popular dish is *picadillos*, made from finely chopped vegetables mixed with beef and served with corn tortillas. Snacks, called *bocas*, consist of small sandwiches, sweet-filled pastries, or tiny tamales. They are often served with the country's rich coffee, which is considered some of the best in the world. Coffee in Costa Rica is prepared either strong and black, made by dripping hot water through a bag of coffee grounds, or as *café con leche*,

Ticos are very proud of their country's natural beauty. One of their favorite weekend destinations is the beach, like this one on the Caribbean coast.

GETTING AROUND IN COSTA RICA

Costa Rica is relatively small, but transportation in the country can be a challenge. Although railway lines were built to serve the coffee and banana industries and still run from San José to Puntarenas on the Pacific coast and to Puerto Limón on the Caribbean side, there are no passenger trains on these routes. Roads also do not offer a great travel option. Roads and freeways around San José are in better shape than others, but most roads and highways in the country have deteriorated due to lack of government funding for repairs and maintenance. Large potholes, along with very bad Tico driving habits, make traveling by car a dangerous proposition. Buses, however, run to even the most remote towns and help to soften the bumpiness of potholes. They are used by most locals as their main means of transportation. By far the best way to get around in Costa Rica is by airplane. The government airline, SANSA, has relatively inexpensive flights to many places throughout the country from San José. The small planes provide a quick and comfortable alternative to long, grueling road trips.

which is coffee mixed with liberal amounts of hot milk and sweetened with lots of sugar.

RADIO, TELEVISION, AND THE INTERNET

Costa Rica, like other developed countries, has a wide variety of radio and television programming that is available nationwide to entertain its citizens. Radio, for example, has long provided a way for Costa Ricans in remote parts of the country to stay in touch with national and international news and events. Today, at least 130 radio stations fill the airwaves with programming that includes talk shows, soap operas, political commentary, comedy, educational programs, and religious shows. Costa Ricans' music is also a large part of radio programming; everything from U.S. pop songs to familiar Caribbean and Latin music can be found on the radio dial. Sports coverage, especially of beloved soccer games, is highly popular as well.

Television, first available in Costa Rica during the 1950s, quickly gained a large following. The country now has a government television station and at least a dozen commercial ones, providing a variety of programming options. These include news, such as the long-running *Telenoticias* (*TV News*) show; sports coverage of soccer games, bicycle races, and swim meets; comedy and game shows; and religious programs. U.S. cable became available in the 1980s, bringing American programs into Costa Rican homes. Satellite dishes are also popular for those who cannot get cable hookups. Costa Ricans can now watch English-language programming—everything from CNN news to ESPN sports coverage to HBO movies. This invasion of American culture into Costa Rica is a concern to some, who see it as replacing local culture and encouraging materialistic values, but others welcome it as a sign of Costa Rica's cosmopolitan nature.

Unrestricted Internet access is similarly available to many Costa Ricans at a relatively low cost. Not all citizens yet have access to this technology, but as of December 2003, 18.7 percent of the population, or about eight hundred thousand Costa Ricans, were surfing the Web.

A woman sells copies of the conservative La Nación, *Costa Rica's largest daily newspaper. Other papers offer alternative political perspectives.*

Print Media

Costa Ricans also have long enjoyed freedom of the press, and an array of newspapers, magazines, and other publications are available in the country. Today, the nation has three main newspapers. The largest daily newspaper, *La Nación*, has a circulation of more than seventy-five thousand and has historically presented a conservative business perspective to its readers. Two other large daily newspapers provide alternative voices. One, *La República*, also with a large circulation, was sympathetic to President Figueres's policies and offers the main ideological counterpart to *La Nación*. An afternoon paper, *La Prensa Libre*, is another progressive publication with significant circulation numbers.

Other print media published in Costa Rica include *Semanario Universidad*, a newspaper published by the University of Costa Rica. It is known for its coverage of international politics and for its progressive political stance. The leading English-language newspaper in Costa Rica is the *Tico Times*. It is largely read by Americans and other foreigners living in the country and offers a nonnative perspective on local and national events. It also provides numerous real estate listings and other information useful for people wanting to move to Costa Rica.

In addition to newspapers, the country also produces a wide variety of magazines and periodicals. These range from tourist magazines to evangelical Christian publications to ecological and scholarly journals. One highly respected publication of scholarly research is *Káñina*, a journal published by the University of Costa Rica. Its issues have included, for example, articles on Costa Rican art, studies of local indigenous cultures, and analyses of Costa Rican literature.

Theater, Literature, and the Arts

On the other hand, Costa Rica has historically not been known for its native or fine arts. Its small size and tiny indigenous population left little in the way of a cultural legacy. Today, however, the arts are becoming very important to the country. Theater, for instance, is one of Costa Ricans' favorite activities, and San José is the center of this arts community. The country's most famous theater is the Teatro Nacional, an architectural treasure built by the coffee elite in San José in 1897. It is now a famous landmark and a venue

COSTA RICA'S *CARRETAS*

Sarchí, a town located in north-central Costa Rica, is the center for production of wooden oxcarts, called *carretas*, which are one of the country's most well-known symbols. In the late 1800s the rustic oxcarts were the most common form of transportation in the countryside, where they were used to transport coffee beans from the interior regions to the port at Puntarenas on the Pacific coast. This journey took as long as fifteen days. In the rainy season, travel time could be very slow since the carts risked getting bogged down in deep mud. To solve this problem, Costa Ricans created a special spokeless wheel for *carretas* that could cut through the mud without getting stuck.

Although these early oxcarts were functional and unpainted, one day a farmer painted an oxcart in bright colors. Since then, oxcart painting has slowly evolved over the decades to become a Costa Rican art form. Contests were held to decide who were the most talented *carretas* artists. Today, oxcarts are no longer used for transportation but have become a common decorative item in the country. Artisans still make full-size oxcarts at their workshops in Sarchí, and smaller versions are offered for sale as souvenirs to tourists. There is even the Oxcart Museum near San José.

An artisan in Sarchí paints an oxcart by hand. The carreta *is a unique Costa Rican folk art form.*

for plays, operas, ballets, music performances by the National Symphony Orchestra, and other cultural activities. Other theater venues operate in the state universities, elsewhere in the San José region, and in other parts of the country.

Not surprising in light of its national emphasis on education and literacy, Costa Rica also has developed a strong literary tradition and produces a wealth of quality fiction and nonfiction, especially from female writers. The first style of literature produced in Costa Rica, *costumbrismo*, consisted of short stories describing typical Costa Rican life. Manuel González Zeledón (also called Magón), wrote weekly vignettes of this type that were published in the Sunday newspapers. Joaquín García Monge made the transition to longer prose by writing the first Costa Rican novel, *El Moto*, in 1900. In the early 1920s María Luisa Carvajal (writing under the name of Carmen Lyra) was the first of a number of female novelists who made their mark on Costa Rican literature. Today, one of the country's most well-known writers is Carmen Jaranjo, a novelist, poet, and short-story writer. Her work has been recognized both in Costa Rica and abroad, and she was nominated in 1998 for the Nobel Prize in literature. She also has been a leader in Costa Rica's arts community, contributing as a government minister of culture and as a founder of important arts organizations such as the national symphony and theater.

In addition, Costa Rica can boast of an array of painters, sculptors, and other artists. These arts are supported by both private donors and the government's Ministry of Culture, Youth, and Sports. The country's painters were influenced largely by European works until the 1920s, when realistic depictions of local life, influenced by *costumbrismo*, began to emerge. This style still can be found, along with more abstract and expressive paintings. Other Costa Rican artists include sculptors who work in both wood and bronze, watercolor painters, and muralists. Today, the growing tourist industry helps to provide a market for many of these artists' works.

Many crafts, too, are available in Costa Rica, from typical Latin tourist items to more elevated art forms. One of the country's most well-known craft items is the *carreta*, a gaily painted oxcart that used to be a common form of transportation. It remains an important symbol of Costa Rica's past and is produced as a souvenir in various sizes, from tiny to life-size carts, for sale to tourists and residents. Another popular craft item is the handcrafted pottery made on the Nicoya Peninsula. The pots are made from local clay and are painted in pre-Columbian Indian colors. In addition, although wood is not as available as it used to be before deforestation, the country's fine hardwoods have produced a tradition of wood-cutters, furniture makers, and woodcarvers. Finely turned Costa Rican bowls and boxes are still a favorite of tourists.

Costa Rica therefore has developed not only politically and economically since its inception but also culturally. Today, it is a rich and interesting land, providing a wealth of leisure and arts activities for all.

6

CHALLENGES FOR COSTA RICA

Costa Rica has already achieved a strong democracy, a stable and relatively prosperous society, and a rich culture, and it benefits from a treasure of natural wonders and resources. The country's biggest challenges in the future will be preserving its democratic values and cultural ideals in the face of growing economic, social, environmental, and political pressures.

ECONOMIC ISSUES

Many experts believe that Costa Rica's most daunting future challenge is economic. On the positive side, Costa Rica has experienced four years of slow economic growth, and in 2003, its economy grew at a healthy 5.6 percent, providing a per-capita income of about ninety-one hundred dollars and an unemployment rate of 6.7 percent. The country's debt also has been significantly reduced since the 1980s. As a Web site affiliated with the Costa Rican–American Chamber of Commerce reports, "The World Bank has given Costa Rica an excellent bill of overall political and economic health. [In 2000] . . . the bank lauded the country as possessing 'one of the most stable and robust' democracies in Latin America. It went on to praise Costa Rica's 'healthy economic growth rate.'"[27]

These economic improvements are largely attributed to Costa Rica's embrace of new private enterprise and free-trade economic concepts promoted by the United States, the International Monetary Fund, and other international organizations. In order to improve efficiency and production, for example, Costa Rican leaders have sold off government-owned sugar and other companies, outsourced the construction of public works, initiated a gradual privatization of the banking system, and allowed health clinics to be managed by private interests. They also have sought to privatize government-run utilities and other industries, such as the ICE (the national electricity company), the INS (the national insurance institute), and RECOPE (the oil and gasoline institute). At the same time, Costa Rica has strongly supported free trade. It has created numerous free-trade zones—areas where foreign businesses are exempted from taxes such as import duties on raw materials and taxes on profits. Most of these foreign investors are also allowed to take their profits out of Costa Rica. Moreover, the country has signed free-trade agreements with the United States, Canada, Mexico, and other regional nations, hoping that these will further stimulate foreign economic investments in Costa Rica. Yet another important strategy has been the introduction of new technologies and export products to wean the country away from its dependence on traditional agricultural exports.

An Intel employee works in a plant near San José. A computer technology company, Intel is the largest exporter in Costa Rica.

TOURISM IN COSTA RICA

Tourism, especially ecotourism (tourism to nature destinations), is a growing industry in Costa Rica. Since the 1980s, the numbers of tourists have doubled, producing a sudden economic boom that generated rising profits for developers and new jobs for Costa Rican workers. Today, the tourism industry is second in size only to the country's electronics industry, and Costa Rica is one of the world's most popular destinations for adventure and nature travel.

Tourism's growth, however, is now being hotly debated in Costa Rica. In the early days, most of Costa Rica's hotels were tiny and run by friendly local people. In recent years, in order to boost tourist profits, the government has permitted the building of numerous large-scale beach resort complexes along its pristine coastlines. Such developments often ignored the country's environmental laws and threatened to destroy the natural environment in exchange for quick tourist dollars. As a result, many Costa Ricans became concerned that the country was embracing mass tourism, similar to the sprawling resorts such as those built in Cancún, Mexico. The most recent indications, however, suggest that Costa Ricans and their leaders now favor an environmentally friendly approach over large-scale development. The era of big resort building has largely ended in the country.

Ecotourists enjoy a trip along on a canal through a rain forest. Costa Rica is a favorite destination for nature lovers.

Many of these efforts have been successful, placing the country on a path toward greater economic stabilization. Once known for its production of coffee, bananas, and beef, for example, Costa Rica has expanded its exports to include many new items, including seafood, plants and flowers, textiles and clothing, pineapples, furniture, and pharmaceutical products. In addition, President Figueres's gamble to attract high-tech manufacturing industries such as Intel, the multinational computer chip maker, seems to have paid off. As travel writers Rob Rachowiecki and John Thompson explain, Intel's factories "fueled the electronics industry to become Costa Rica's top dollar earner in 1998."[28] Since then, the industry has remained strong and other manufacturing companies have also been brought into the country, among them pharmaceutical giant Procter and Gamble, which built a large administrative center in Costa Rica, and health care product manufacturers Abbott Laboratories and Baxter Healthcare. As a result, manufacturing and related industries now produce significantly more income than agriculture. Tourism is another relatively new industry that has recently recorded significant growth and is expected to grow more in the future. The number of tourists visiting Costa Rica has more than doubled from about 376,000 in 1989 to close to a million per year today. Tourism, like manufacturing, now earns the country more in revenues than its traditional agricultural exports.

Yet Costa Rica today still grapples with a large foreign debt and economic problems created by overspending and deficit budgets. As the U.S. State Department explains, "Controlling the budget deficit remains the single-biggest challenge for the country's economic policymakers."[29] In 2003, as in previous years, a large part (more than 18 percent) of the national budget was financed by public borrowing. Indeed, just paying the interest on the country's debt cost Costa Rica more than 30 percent of the government's total revenues in 2003. Costa Rica's dependence on foreign, mostly U.S., imports also remains a concern since imports continue to outnumber Costa Rican exports to the United States and other countries. Greater expansion of exports, economists say, is key to increasing Costa Rica's long-term economic wealth and well-being. Another problem inhibiting economic growth is Costa Rica's deteriorating roads, ports, and railroad lines. Investment in these infrastructure systems is crucial to providing adequate transportation for commerce and necessary to attract foreign businesses. The country's pattern of deficit spending and debt, however, has reduced the resources available to the country for these needed economic improvements.

In addition, some of Costa Rica's economic growth strategies have come under serious criticism at home. Citizen protests, for example, have slowed progress on privatization and social-service budget cuts and have forced the government to proceed slowly and carefully on these reforms. In addition, some economists worry that much of the growth in tourism and manufacturing industries has been fueled mostly by the United States. As the U.S. State Department notes, "The U.S. accounts for over half of Costa Rica's tourism and more than two-thirds of its foreign investment."[30] This, critics say, makes Costa Rica overly dependent on the United States. Other experts question the value of all foreign-owned investments since the benefits granted to foreign companies typically do not require profits to be reinvested in Costa Rica. Supporters of the government's policies disagree, pointing to the value of good jobs created by such enterprises and the funds pumped into Costa Rica's economy from their purchase of electricity and other local prod-

In protest against free-trade negotiations with the United States, a Costa Rican waves a homemade U.S. flag featuring anti-American graffiti.

ucts and services. In addition, government officials hope that their policies will spur the development of local businesses and investments that eventually will create real wealth for Costa Rica.

Most observers, however, are optimistic that Costa Rica's economy will continue to improve, if only because the country has so many resources and advantages in the world economy. Costa Rica, unlike many less-developed nations, has an educated population, a history of responsible political leadership, and a reputation as a stable place for economic investment and development. It also has important natural resources, such as the country's mountainous terrain and abundant rainfall; these assets provide cheap hydroelectric power and make Costa Rica largely self-sufficient in most energy needs and a future exporter of electricity. The country, too, has good agricultural land, a beautiful environment that attracts a growing number of tourists, and an increasing dedication to managing and sustaining these environmental resources. If Costa Rica can continue to pay down its debt, get a handle on government expenditures, and continue developing its private industries, most observers predict that the country will eventually be able to pull out of its tight economic straits.

SOCIAL ISSUES

Whether Costa Rica can recover economically without destroying its social welfare traditions, however, is another very real challenge for the country. Austerity programs designed to combat economic problems by cutting spending have forced cutbacks in the country's education and social safety net. Observers say quality has suffered in schools, and medicines are in short supply. New policies have also caused increases in poverty and unemployment. Privatization of state-owned businesses and cutbacks in government spending, for example, have caused many workers to be laid off and have shrunk the salaries and pensions of public employees. Meanwhile, workers in traditional industries, such as banana plantations, have also lost their jobs due to increased competition from other countries and decreased production. The shift from a state-run economy to a free-market and free-trade economy has truly been difficult for many affected workers in Costa Rica.

Costa Ricans' displeasure with the government's new economic policies finally erupted in 2000, when Costa Rican president Rodriguez sought to privatize the state-owned telecommunications and electricity utility, ICE. In March of that year, Costa Rica was shaken by a series of mass strikes and protests by workers, students, and peasants. Police reacted to the first week of nationwide demonstrations with violence, provoking outrage among a public devoted to peaceful relations. The next day, half a million people marched in peaceful demonstrations protesting both the ICE policy and the violence, leading to a three-week-long general strike marked by constant marches, blockades, and traffic stoppages. The protesters used this time to argue that the privatization of ICE would lead to much higher electric rates and more job losses. Many protesters felt that such a policy amounted to selling the country to foreign interests. As reporter Kim Alphandary documented, "The resounding cry heard everywhere [during the marches] was 'Costa Rica is not for sale!'"[31] The widespread civil unrest was resolved only when President Rodriguez agreed to suspend the ICE privatization plan and establish a commission to study other options. In May 2003, however, national strikes again shook the country when energy and telecommunications workers protested President Abel Pacheco's continuation of privatization plans. At the same time, a strike by teachers protested delays in payment of salaries and government cuts in education and pensions.

Adding to these problems of civil unrest over privatization and austerity cutbacks is a growing Costa Rican population, fueled by a relatively high birthrate and an influx of immigrants from other parts of Central America. The country's population stood at about 2.8 million people in 1987; today, it has grown to 3.96 million. This increase in population has further burdened the country's education and social service programs just at the time when the country can least afford it. The increases in population, many observers claim, have also contributed to a growing crime wave that threatens Costa Rica's cultural stability and peace.

Some experts even believe that the nation's strong ethic of providing for its people is slowly crumbling without adequate resources. As professor Bruce M. Wilson explains, "The social democratic model that defined Costa Rica from the

end of the civil war until the 1980s . . . , if not dead, is at least muted."[32] Whether the government can improve the economy while protecting the core of its education and social programs remains to be seen.

National strikes disrupted Costa Rican society in 2003. Here, thousands of striking teachers march through the streets of San José with demands for a better retirement plan.

ENVIRONMENTAL CONCERNS

Recent decades have also brought environmental challenges for Costa Rica. The country's early economic development resulted in large tracts of native dry forests and rain forests being cut down for farmland and pastures. This was particularly true in the highlands, which are perfect for growing coffee, and the Pacific lowlands, where cattle ranching has made beef a major export. The introduction of cattle ranching has

CONSERVATION OF COSTA RICA'S NATURAL RESOURCES

Although Costa Rica has experienced a high rate of deforestation, the country also has one of the world's best conservation records. This is explained by the fact that Costa Rica has managed to protect more of its land than almost any other country in the world. Beginning in the 1970s, Costa Ricans began to understand that their wilderness was unique and that it was being threatened by overdevelopment. In response, the government created a national park and forest reserve system that set aside more than 10 percent of the country's land for parks and another 17 percent as forests and wildlife reserves. Today, this system includes twenty-four national parks, ten biological reserves, twelve forest reserves, and thirty-four wildlife refuges. In addition to protecting flora and fauna, these reserves preserve the country's soils and water sources and provide Costa Ricans and visitors the chance to admire and study the wonders of nature. The government also has sought to control the logging of valuable hardwoods from its forests and has promoted reforestation. Yet despite these efforts, Costa Rica's forests continue to be lost to farmers, ranchers, and illegal logging faster than anywhere else in the Western Hemisphere.

A tourist snaps a picture in a cloud forest preserve. Costa Rica is dedicated to protecting its natural resources.

caused the most environmental damage because, as Christopher P. Baker notes, ranching "takes up [as pastureland] more than 20 times the amount of land devoted to bananas and coffee."[33] Logging activities posed yet another threat to the hardwood forests. As a result, by the 1990s forests that had once covered most of the country existed on only about 8 percent of Costa Rica's territory. Conservationists feared that, at this rate, almost all the country's forests could be gone in just a few decades.

In response to this legacy of environmental destruction, the government in recent years has enacted legislation to protect the remaining forested areas, has sought to restrict logging activities, and has promoted reforestation. These efforts have helped somewhat, but they also have been beset by problems, including a lack of funding caused by economic austerity policies. At the same time, Costa Rica faces continuing pressures to improve the country's economy at the cost of further damage to the environment. For example, the emphasis on tourism to jumpstart the economy has threatened to destroy Costa Rica's natural environment, with large resorts and hotels being built in disregard of the country's environmental laws. Environmentalists also charge that bribes are paid to government officials by developers, and they say that the country is badly in need of a master development plan and enhanced enforcement efforts to ensure against an environmental catastrophe.

These concerns seem to be resulting in a renewed emphasis on environmental protections and sustainable development. The government has begun to license tourist companies, and it placed quotas on the number of visitors to national parks. Most recently, President Pacheco has declared a moratorium on new open-pit mining projects, has cracked down on illegal logging, and has designated new national parkland. Government officials also, for environmental reasons, recently prohibited the U.S.-based oil company Harken from drilling for oil along the Caribbean coast. President Pacheco has even proposed including environmental guarantees in the Costa Rican constitution in order to establish the public's right to a healthy environment and provide government enforcement of that right. Many hope this enhanced focus on the environment will help save the country's priceless ecosystems from destructive development. Ironically, enforcement of environmental protections may depend on economic development—the very thing that historically has most threatened the country's ecology—since enforcement of environmental policies depends on adequate funding that can come only from new economic gains.

PRESERVING DEMOCRACY

Other challenging issues arising in Costa Rica in recent years have involved threats to the country's sacred democratic system. Despite the country's popular image as a model of democracy, government corruption is now a growing problem. Observers say nepotism and cronyism (the hiring of and giving benefits to family and friends) are entrenched in the country's politics, resulting in unfair government contract awards and other types of government fraud that deplete the country's scarce revenues. One recent scandal, for example, involved claims that the government has overpaid private electricity generators, some of which were owned by politicians.

The corruption scandals are causing Ticos to become disillusioned with the country's two main parties—the National Liberation Party (PLN) and the Social Christian Unity Party (PUSC)—and are giving new parties a boost in recent elections. In the 2002 elections, for example, a new third-party candidate, Otton Solis, captured 26 percent of the total vote, forcing a run-off election that eventually brought President Pacheco to power. In the same 2002 elections, a third party, the Civic Action Party, won a quarter of the votes in the legislature, shifting the balance of power there into a three-way split. Notably, Solis campaigned against corruption, and the strength of his support revealed the high level of voter concern over political corruption. Voter disillusionment with politics was also evident in the fact that only 69 percent of voters went to the polls, the smallest number since 1958.

Since the 2002 elections, even more scandals have come to light. In fact, two PUSC leaders and former presidents—Rafael Calderón and Miguel Rodríguez—were jailed in 2004 on corruption charges. Former President José Figueres, of the PLN, is also suspected of involvement in corruption. Rodolfo Cerdas, a political analyst in Costa Rica, explained the depth of public concern over these political events: "At this time [November 2004], the parties of the country are in crisis, and it is the moment for new political movements. There is a divorce between the political parties and the people."[34]

Another threat to Costa Rica's democracy, many experts say, is a growing government bureaucracy that is becoming unresponsive to the nation's needs. Today, about 25 percent of the Costa Rican population, or about one in every four working people, are employed by the government. The vast numbers of public employees were hired to run the country's many social welfare programs, but they are so entrenched and unresponsive that even the simplest interaction with the government often involves hours of waiting in long lines. Public employees also have historically been paid good

PRESIDENT PACHECO AND CORRUPTION

Abel Pacheco won a tightly contested run-off presidential election in April 2002. Since then, Pacheco has faced growing citizen opposition. In 2003, for example, electrical and telecommunications workers staged a strike over his plans to privatize the country's electric utility company, and teachers protested cuts in their pensions. Pacheco lost even more public support in 2003 when allegations arose accusing him of financing his campaign illegally with funds from foreign business interests. Specifically, Pacheco's presidential campaign reportedly received donations from French telecommunications company Alcatel, a company accused of offering bribes to Costa Rican government officials as rewards for government contracts. Later, in 2004, Pacheco was accused of accepting similar campaign funds from the government of Taiwan. The reports about Pacheco surfaced amid a storm of corruption scandals involving several past presidents. Public outrage concerning the scandals boiled over when thousands of Costa Ricans staged a

march against corruption in San José in October 2004. President Pacheco tried to join the march but was booed, heckled, and forced to leave. Although he has vowed not to resign, many observers expect Pacheco to be replaced by a new president in 2006.

An angry Costa Rican takes to the streets in protest of corruption scandals involving President Pacheco and other officials in 2004.

wages and given high job security and generous pensions—
a generosity that depletes a large proportion of the country's
now limited revenues. In addition, the large numbers of public employees have created a vocal citizen opposition to government cutbacks, making it difficult for Costa Rican
politicians to address problems. Many Costa Ricans fear that
their country could suffer the same fate as Uruguay, another
model democracy whose economy and government crum-
bled into dictatorship in 1973 due to its inability to pay for
generous social benefits and a large government bureaucracy.

Other political issues have included criticism of the 1969
constitutional provision that prohibits second terms for
presidents and legislators. Critics say this policy destroyed
accountability and worked against effective government because politicians knew they would not be running for reelection. Politicians could therefore promise whatever they
wanted to get elected, but they often did not implement
these promises once in office. In addition, elections have often been followed by political appointments and other rewards to supporters without worries about losing future
votes. In April 2003, however, Costa Rica's Supreme Court annulled the 1969 amendment, reinstating the right of former
presidents to run for reelection. The ruling paves the way for
former presidents, such as the highly popular President Oscar Arias, to run for office in the 2006 presidential elections.

To continue its reputation as a stable democracy, therefore, Costa Rica may need to revise parts of its democratic
system and restore the public's faith in politics and government. Despite setbacks, experts hope that the country's reasonable leaders and educated populace will eventually be
able to repair the damage to the country's democracy. If
Costa Rica can solve some of these systemic political and
economic problems, adapt its social welfare bureaucracy to
reasonable government spending restraints, and avoid destruction of its precious environmental resources, it will
likely continue to reign as an oasis of freedom, peace, and
prosperity in Central America.

FACTS ABOUT
COSTA RICA

GEOGRAPHY

Location: Central America, bordering both the Caribbean Sea and the North Pacific Ocean, between Nicaragua and Panama

Area:

Total: 19,730 square miles

Land: 19,560 square miles

Water: 170 square miles

Area comparative: Slightly smaller than West Virginia

Border countries: Nicaragua and Panama

Coastline: 800 miles

Climate: Tropical and subtropical; dry season (December to April); rainy season (May to November); cooler in highlands

Terrain: Coastal plains separated by rugged mountains that include over 100 volcanic cones, of which several are major volcanoes

Natural resources: Hydropower

Land use:

Arable land: 4.41 percent

Permanent crops: 5.88 percent

Other: 89.71 percent (1998 estimate)

Natural hazards: Occasional earthquakes; hurricanes along Caribbean coast; frequent flooding of lowlands at onset of rainy season and landslides; active volcanoes

Environmental issues: Deforestation and land use change, largely a result of the clearing of land for cattle ranching and agriculture; soil erosion; coastal marine pollution; fisheries protection; solid waste management; air pollution

PEOPLE

Population: 3,956,507 (2004 est.)

Age structure:

0–14 years: 40.6 percent (male 56,530; female 54,322)

15–64 years: 55.8 percent (male 77,118; female 75,309)

65 years and over: 3.5 percent (male 4,674; female 4,992) (2004 est.)   91

Birthrate: 18.99 births/1,000 population (2004 est.)

Death rate: 4.32 deaths/1,000 population (2004 est.)

Infant mortality rate: 10.26 deaths/1,000 live births (2004 est.)

Life expectancy:

    Total population: 76.63 years

    Male: 74.07 years

    Female: 79.33 years (2004 est.)

Fertility rate: 2.33 children born/woman (2004 est.)

Ethnic groups:

    White (including mestizo): 94 percent

    Black: 3 percent

    Amerindian: 1 percent

    Chinese: 1 percent

    Other: 1 percent

Religions:

    Roman Catholic: 76.3 percent

    Evangelical: 13.7 percent

    Jehovah's Witnesses: 1.3 percent

    Protestant: 0.7 percent

    Other: 4.8 percent

    None: 3.2 percent

Languages: Spanish (official) and English

Literacy rate for those age 15 and over:

    Total population: 96 percent

    Male: 95.9 percent

    Female: 96.1 percent (2003 est.)

GOVERNMENT

Country name: Republic of Costa Rica

Form of government: Democratic republic

Capital: San José

Administrative divisions: 7 provinces: Alajuela, Cartago, Guanacaste, Heredia, Limón, Puntarenas, San José

National holiday: Independence Day, September 15

Date of independence: September 15, 1821 (from Spain)

Constitution: November 7, 1949

Legal system: Based on Spanish civil law system; judicial review of legislative acts in the Supreme Court; has accepted compulsory International Court of Justice jurisdiction

Suffrage: 18 years of age, universal and compulsory

Executive branch: Chief of state, President Abel Pacheco (since May 8, 2002)(Note: the president is both the chief of state and the head of government); First Vice President Lineth Saborio (since May 2002);

Second Vice President Luis Fishman (since May 2002); cabinet—selected by the president; elections—president and vice presidents elected on the same ticket by popular vote for four-year terms; election last held February 3, 2002; run-off election held April 7, 2002; next election to be held February 2006

Legislative branch: Unicameral Legislative Assembly—57 seats; members are elected by direct, popular vote to serve four-year terms; elections last held February 3, 2002; next elections to be held February 2006; 2002 election results: seats by party—PUSC (Social Christian Unity Party) 19, PLN (National Liberation Party) 17, PAC (Citizens' Action Party) 14, PML (Libertarian Movement Party) 6, PRC (Costa Rican Renovation Party) 1

Judicial branch: Supreme Court—22 justices are elected for eight-year terms by the Legislative Assembly

ECONOMY

Gross domestic product (GDP): $35.34 billion (2003 est.)

Real growth: 5.6 percent (2003 est.)

GDP per capita: $9,100 (2003 est.)

GDP composition: agriculture, 8.5 percent; industry, 29.4 percent; services, 62.1 percent (2003 est.)

Labor force: 1.758 million (2003 est.)

Industries: Microprocessors, food processing, textiles and clothing, construction materials, fertilizer, plastic products

Agriculture products: Coffee, pineapples, bananas, sugar, corn, rice, beans, potatoes, beef, and timber

Exports: $6.176 billion (2003 est.)

Imports: $5.057 billion (2003 est.)

Debt: $5.366 billion (2001 est.)

Currency: Costa Rican colón

NOTES

CHAPTER 1: LAND OF BEAUTY

1. Richard Biesanz, Karen Zubris Biesanz, and Mavis Hiltunen Biesanz, *The Costa Ricans*. Prospect Heights, IL: Waveland, 1988, p. 1.

2. Christopher P. Baker, *Costa Rica Handbook*. Chico, CA: Moon, 1999, p. 500.

3. Christopher P. Baker, "Ecosystems," Photo Net. www.photo.net/cr/moon/ecosystems.html.

CHAPTER 2: COSTA RICA'S BEGINNINGS

4. Bruce M. Wilson, *Costa Rica: Politics, Economics, and Democracy*. Boulder, CO: Lynne Rienner, 1998, p. 11.

5. Biesanz, Biesanz, and Biesanz, *The Costa Ricans*, p. 16.

6. Biesanz, Biesanz, and Biesanz, *The Costa Ricans*, p. 20.

7. Wilson, *Costa Rica*, p. 31.

8. Biesanz, Biesanz, and Biesanz, *The Costa Ricans*, p. 28.

9. Marc Edelman and Joanne Kenen, eds., *Costa Rica Reader*. New York: Grove Weidenfeld, 1989, p. 88.

CHAPTER 3: DEMOCRATIC COSTA RICA

10. Wilson, *Costa Rica*, p. 41.

11. Edelman and Kenen, *Costa Rica Reader*, p. 127.

12. Wilson, *Costa Rica*, p. 116.

13. Biesanz, Biesanz, and Biesanz, *The Costa Ricans*, p. 177.

14. Quoted in Baker, *Costa Rica Handbook*, p. 79.

CHAPTER 4: COSTA RICAN SOCIETY

15. Baker, *Costa Rica Handbook*, p. 92.

16. Charlene Helmuth, *Culture and Customs of Costa Rica*. Westport, CT: Greenwood, 2000, p. 61.

17. Baker, *Costa Rica Handbook*, p 90.

18. Biesanz, Biesanz, and Biesanz, *The Costa Ricans*, p. 67.

19. Biesanz, Biesanz, and Biesanz, *The Costa Ricans*, p. 48.

20. Baker, *Costa Rica Handbook*, p 93.

21. Helmuth, *Culture and Customs of Costa Rica*, p. 51.

22. Helmuth, *Culture and Customs of Costa Rica*, pp. 29–30.

23. Isabel de Bertodano, "The Costa Rican Health System: Low Cost, High Value," *Bulletin of the World Health Organization*, August 2003, vol. 81, iss. 8, p. 6(2).

CHAPTER 5: ARTS AND LEISURE

24. Helmuth, *Culture and Customs of Costa Rica*, p. 72.

25. Baker, *Costa Rica Handbook*, p. 123.

26. Helmuth, *Culture and Customs of Costa Rica*, p. 73.

CHAPTER 6: CHALLENGES FOR COSTA RICA

27. Doing Business in Costa Rica, "Doing Business in Costa Rica," 2000. www.businesscostarica.com.

28. Rob Rachowiecki and John Thompson, *Costa Rica*. Hawthorn, Australia: Lonely Planet, 2000, p. 30.

29. U.S. Department of State, Bureau of Western Hemisphere Affairs, "Background Note: Costa Rica," August 2004. www.state.gov/r/pa/ei/bgn/2019.htm.

30. U.S. Department of State, Bureau of Western Hemisphere Affairs, "Background Note: Costa Rica."

31. Kim Alphandary, "Report from Costa Rica on Mass Protests Against Privatization of State-Owned Utilities," World Socialist Web Site. April 15, 2000. www.wsws.org/articles/2000/apr2000/cr-a15.shtml.

32. Wilson, *Costa Rica*, pp.161–62.

33. Baker, *Costa Rica Handbook*, p. 25.

34. Quoted in Steven J. Barry, "Scandals Take Political Toll," *Tico Times Online*, November 5–11 weekly edition. www.ticotimes.net/newsbriefs.htm.

CHRONOLOGY

12,000 B.C.
Nomadic hunters travel to the area now called Costa Rica.

A.D. 1502
Spanish explorer Christopher Columbus visits the area.
Spain calls it Costa Rica ("Rich Coast") and soon claims it as
part of the Spanish colonial empire in Central America.

1561
Spain establishes an inland settlement in the Central Valley
at Cartago.

1808
Coffee is introduced into Costa Rica and becomes the principal crop.

1821
Central America, including Costa Rica, gains independence
from Spain.

1823
Costa Rica joins the United Provinces of Central America, a
group of Central American countries that also includes El
Salvador, Guatemala, Honduras, and Nicaragua.

1824
Costa Rica elects a congress and chooses its first leader,
Juan Mora Fernández.

1834
A new head of state, Braulio Carrillo Colina, is elected; in
1838 he seizes control of the government and rules as a dictator.

1842
Francisco Morazán becomes Costa Rica's leader but is
quickly overthrown. During the next several years, multiple
leaders hold office.

1847

Costa Rica selects José María Castro Madriz as the country's first president.

1849

Juan Rafael Mora Porras becomes Costa Rica's president.

1856

Under the leadership of President Mora, Costa Rica resists an invasion by troops sent by William Walker, a U.S. adventurer who had taken over the government of Nicaragua in 1855.

1870

Tomás Guardia Gutiérrez is elected and acts to weaken the power of the coffee barons. He also encourages the construction of the country's first railroad.

1874

Banana cultivation begins in Costa Rica.

1882

President Guardia dies and a group of young men, called "the Generation of 1889," push for social change.

1889

A candidate not supported by the coffee elites, José Joaquín Rodríguez Zeledón, becomes president.

1917

Frederico Tinoco Granados becomes president in a coup and conducts a repressive regime until he is forced to resign in 1918.

1940–1948

President Rafael Ángel Calderón Guardia is elected and implements social reforms, including recognition of workers rights and minimum wages. Calderón's policies are continued under a succeeding president, Teodoro Picado Mikalski.

1948

Civil war erupts over a disputed presidential election result for Rafael Otilio Ulate Blanco, but a cease-fire agreement is negotiated after several months; José Figueres Ferrer takes control of the government through a revolutionary junta and issues numerous decrees, beginning an ambitious social welfare program and abolishing the armed forces.

1949
A new constitution is adopted that provides for fair elections and gives women and blacks the right to vote. Ulate becomes president.

1978
Rodrigo Carazo Odio is elected president and presides over a sharp deterioration in the economy.

1982
PLN candidate Luis Alberto Monge Álvarez is elected president and introduces a harsh austerity program.

1985
U.S.-trained antiguerrilla forces, called Contras, begin operating in Costa Rica to oppose Nicaragua's Sandinista government.

1986
PLN candidate Oscar Arias Sánchez is elected president.

1987
Leaders of Nicaragua, El Salvador, Guatemala, and Honduras sign a peace plan proposed by President Arias; Arias wins the Nobel Peace Prize.

1990
PUSC candidate Rafael Calderón Fournier (son of the former president) is elected president.

1994
PLN candidate José María Figueres Olsen (son of the former president) is elected president. Intel, a giant computer chip manufacturer, builds a large assembly plant in Costa Rica.

1998
PUSC candidate Miguel Ángel Rodriguez Echeverría is elected president.

2000
Costa Rican workers protest President Rodriguez's plan to privatize the state-owned telecommunications and electricity utility, ICE.

2002

PUSC candidate Abel Pacheco de la Espriella is elected president in a run-off election.

2003

Energy and telecommunications workers strike over President Pacheco's privatization plans; teachers strike over problems in paying their salaries and budget cuts.

2004

Concern over corruption mounts as two former presidents —Rafael Calderón and Miguel Rodriguez—are jailed for corruption. Former president José Figueres is investigated for involvement in corruption, and President Abel Pacheco is accused of illegal campaign financing.

FOR FURTHER READING

BOOKS

Ronnie Cummins, *Children of the World: Costa Rica.* Milwaukee: Gareth Stevens Children's, 1990. This book follows the life of a farm girl from Costa Rica, describing her family, school, and community. The book also provides information about Costa Rica's history, government, geography, religion, art, and society.

Erin Foley, *Cultures of the World: Costa Rica.* New York: Marshal Cavendish, 1997. A young-adult book that provides an overview of Costa Rica, including geography, history, government, economy, lifestyle, religion, and many other topics.

Tracey West, *Costa Rica.* Minneapolis: Carolrhoda, 1999. An easy-to-read overview of Costa Rica, with large print and numerous photos, maps, and graphics.

WEB SITES

Centralamerica.com (http://centralamerica.com/cr/info /index.htm). A travel Web site that provides background on Costa Rica's history, climate, geography, and government as well as information about tourist attractions and activities.

Tico Times (www.ticotimes.net). The Web site for Costa Rica's leading English-language newspaper, covering news, business, tourism, and cultural developments in Costa Rica and Central America.

U.S. Central Intelligence Agency (CIA) (www.cia.gov/cia/ publications/factbook/geos/cs.html). This U.S. government Web site gives geographical, political, economic, and other information on Costa Rica.

U.S. Department of State (http://travel.state.gov/travel/ costa_rica.html). A U.S. government Web site providing practical information and travel warnings for people who plan to visit Costa Rica.

WORKS CONSULTED

BOOKS

Christopher P. Baker, *Costa Rica Handbook*. Chico, CA: Moon, 1999. A travel handbook on Costa Rica with discussions of its geography, climate, ecosystems, wildlife, history, government, economy, and people.

Richard Biesanz, Karen Zubris Biesanz, and Mavis Hiltunen Biesanz, *The Costa Ricans*. Prospect Heights, IL: Waveland, 1988. A comprehensive overview of Costa Rica detailing the country's history, society, culture, and government.

Marc Edelman and Joanne Kenen, eds., *Costa Rica Reader*. New York: Grove Weidenfeld, 1989. A volume of essays and speeches from noted scholars and writers providing a wide range of perspectives on Costa Rica's history, economy, politics, society, and government.

Charlene Helmuth, *Culture and Customs of Costa Rica*. Westport, CT: Greenwood, 2000. A scholarly but readable introduction to Costa Rica, with a focus on its social customs, culture, leisure activities, and arts.

Rob Rachowiecki and John Thompson, *Costa Rica*. Hawthorn, Australia: Lonely Planet, 2000. A travel book about Costa Rica containing overviews of its history, geography, climate, environment, national parks, government, economy, people, and society.

Bruce M. Wilson, *Costa Rica: Politics, Economics, and Democracy*. Boulder, CO: Lynne Rienner, 1998. A scholarly discussion of Costa Rica's political history, from colonial times to the late 1990s.

PERIODICALS

Isabel de Bertodano, "The Costa Rican Health System: Low Cost, High Value," *Bulletin of the World Health Organization.* August 2003, vol. 81, iss. 8.

Brad Stone, "A Silicon Republic: A Few Years Ago, Costa Rica Was Known Mainly for Its Bananas. Then the World's Biggest Semiconductor Maker Came Calling. Lessons from the High-Tech Frontier," *Newsweek*, August 28, 2000.

Dave Taylor, "Costa Rica Launches Environmental Initiatives," *World Watch*, September/October 2002, vol. 15, iss. 5.

Joyce Gregory Wyels, "The Challenge to Paternalism; Costa Rica's Election," *Economist*, April 6, 2002.

———, "Common Ground for Farmers and Forests: Alarmed by Signs of Extensive Deforestation over the Past Decades, Groups in Costa Rica Are Developing Programs That Combine Ecological Awareness and Sustainable Agriculture," *Americas*, March/April 2003, vol. 55, iss. 2.

INTERNET SOURCES

Janne Abullarade, "Costa Rica Electrical Workers Strike, Block Government Attempt to Privatize Utility," *Militant*, August 18, 2003, vol. 67, no. 28. www.themilitant.com/2003/6728/672853.html.

Kim Alphandary, "Report from Costa Rica on Mass Protests Against Privatization of State-Owned Utilities," World Socialist Web Site, April 15, 2000. www.wsws.org/articles/2000/apr2000/cr-a15.shtml.

A.M. Costa Rica, "President Pacheco Offers Abundance of Proposals," May 9, 2002. www.amcostarica.com/050902.htm.

Christopher P. Baker, "Ecosystems," Photo Net. www.photo.net/cr/moon/ecosystems.html.

Steven J. Barry, "Scandals Take Political Toll," *Tico Times Online*, November 5–11 weekly edition. www.ticotimes.net/newsbriefs.htm.

BBC News, "Country Profile: Costa Rica," October 30, 2004. http://news.bbc.co.uk/l/low/world/americas/country_ profiles/1166587.stm.

Costa Rica Tourism and Travel Bureau, "Monteverde," November 12, 2002. www.costaricabureau.com/monteverde.htm.

Doing Business in Costa Rica, "Doing Business in Costa Rica," 2000. www.businesscostarica.com.

Freedom House, "Costa Rica," September 9, 2004. www.free domhouse.org/research/freeworld/2004/countryratings/ costarica.htm.

Global Volunteers, "Costa Rica Geography: Scenic and Ecological Wonders," 2003. www.globalvolunteers.org/1main/ costarica/costaricageography.htm.

Alejandra Herranz, "Environment Proposed for Costa Rican Constitution," Green Cross International, September 20, 2002. www.gci.ch/Communication/DigitalForum/digi forum/ARTICLES/article2002/environmentpro.html.

Info Costa Rica, "Guanacaste," 2000. www.infocostarica. com/places/guanacaste.html.

———, "Natural Phenomena: Earthquakes, Floods, etc." 2000. www.infocostarica.com/nature/phenomena.html.

Rebecca Kimitch, "Pacheco Booed, Three Arrested in March Against Corruption," *Tico Times Online*, October 13, 2004. www.ticotimes.net/dailyarchive/2004_10/daily_10_13_04 .htm#story1.

Pablo Sanchez, "Workers' Struggles in Costa Rica," June 6, 2003. www.marxist.com/Latinam/costarica_0603.html.

Tico Times Online, "Supreme Court Reinstates Reelection," April 7, 2003. www.ticotimes.net/dailyarchive/2003_04/ week2/04_07_03.htm#story_one.

U.S. Department of State, Bureau of Western Hemisphere Affairs, "Background Note: Costa Rica," August 2004. www. state.gov/r/pa/ei/bgn/2019.htm.

U.S. Embassy, Office of the U.S. Trade Representative, "U.S.

and Costa Rica Reach Agreement on Free Trade," January 25, 2004. http://usembassy.or.cr/Cafta/040125.html.

Viva Costa Rica, "Story of William Walker," 2003. www.viva costarica.com/costa-rica-information/history-of-costa-rica-4.html.

INDEX

Picture Credits

Cover: © age/footstock/Superstock
AP Wide World Photos, 44, 58, 67, 73, 79
Jeffrey Arguedas/EPA/Landov, 48
© Bettmann/CORBIS, 28, 35, 38, 41, 43
Everett Kennedy Brown/EPA/Landov, 46
Lee Foster/Lonely Planet Images, 17, 25
© Bill Gentile/CORBIS, 47
© Getty Images, 33
Ralph Lee Hopkins/Lonely Planet Images, 22
© Dave G. Hauser/CORBIS, 75
© Buddy Mays/CORBIS, 21
© Michael Maslan Historical Photos/CORBIS, 32
© Martin Rogers/CORBIS, 8, 18, 61, 62, 65, 68, 71
© Carmen Redondo/CORBIS, 55
Reuters/Landov, 7, 52
Stephen Saks/Lonely Planet Images, 80
© Juan Carlos Ulate/Reuters/CORBIS, 27, 57
Patricia Ugalde/EPA/Landov, 85
Juan Carlos Ulate/Reuters/Landov, 82, 89
© Brian A. Vikander/CORBIS, 86
Brent Winebrenner/Lonely Planet Images, 13
Steve Zmina, 11, 15

ABOUT THE AUTHOR

Debra A. Miller is a writer and a lawyer with a passion for current events and history. She began her law career in Washington, D.C., where she worked on legislative, policy, and legal matters in government, public interest, and private law firm positions. She now lives with her husband in Encinitas, California. She has written and edited publications for legal publishers as well as numerous books and anthologies on historical and political topics.